HURRICANE

These are the people who live on the small island of Manukura in the South Pacific, and the story of a devastating hurricane that hits the island ...

DR. KERSAINT, French medical officer of the islands

FATHER PAUL, the kind-hearted priest, who truly loves the island and its people

CAPTAIN NAGLE, an English captain and trader who sails the South Seas

DE LAAGE, the French consul, a fair but rigid government official

MADAME DE LAAGE, his beautiful and sympathetic wife

TERANGI, a decidedly superior young islander who has been unjustly imprisoned, and now has escaped to return to Manukura' to try to flee with his wife and child

---

"A masterpiece written within our time. The story is timeless, universal and, in the best sense, human. If you miss this tale you are cheating no one but yourself."

—Sterling North

D0645926

Dino De Laurentiis Presents

"Hurricane"

Starring Jason Robards Mia Farrow

Max Von Sydow Trevor Howard

Timothy Bottoms

and introducing Dayton Ka'ne

Produced by Dino De Laurentiis

Directed by Jan Troell

Screenplay by Lorenzo Semple, Jr.

Executive Producer Lorenzo Semple, Jr.

Famous Films Productions N.V.

A Paramount Release

The Motion Picture is suggested
by the book HURRICANE by
Charles Nordhoff and James Hall

HURRICANE

By Charles Nordhoff and James Norman Hall

BANTAM BOOKS · TORONTO · NEW YORK · LONDON

*This low-priced Bantam Book
has been completely reset in a type face
designed for easy reading, and was printed
from new plates. It contains the complete
text of the original hard-cover edition.*
NOT ONE WORD HAS BEEN OMITTED.

🦅

HURRICANE
*A Bantam Book / published by arrangement with Little,
Brown & Co.*

PRINTING HISTORY
*Little, Brown & Co. edition published February 1936
28 printings through February 1969
Bantam edition / April 1979*

Bantam Books are published by Bantam Books, Inc. Its trademark, consisting of the words "Bantam Books" and the portrayal of a bantam, is Registered in U.S. Patent and Trademark Office and in other countries. Marca Registrada. Bantam Books, Inc., 666 Fifth Avenue, New York, New York 10019.

PRINTED IN THE UNITED STATES OF AMERICA

To our old friend
EDWARD WEEKS

Chapter

1

Scattered over a thousand miles of ocean in the eastern tropical Pacific, below the Equator, lies a vast collection of coral islands extending in a general northwesterly, southeasterly direction across ten degrees of latitude. Seventy-eight atolls, surf-battered dikes of coral, enclosing lagoons, make up this barrier to the steady westward roll of the sea. Some of the lagoons are scarcely more than salt-water ponds; others, like those of Rangiroa and Fakarava, are as much as fifty miles long by twenty or thirty across. The motu, or islets, composing the land, are threaded at wide intervals on the encircling reef. The smaller ones are frequented by sea fowl which nest in the pandanus trees and among the fronds of scattered coconut palms. Others, enchantingly green and restful to sea-weary eyes, follow the curve of the reef for many miles, sloping away over the arc of the world until they are lost to view. But whatever their extent, one feature is common to all: they are mere fringes of land seldom more than a quarter of a mile in width, and rising only a few feet above the sea which seems always on the point of overwhelming them.

There is no other group of islands so remote from any continent. The inhabitants, few in number, are Polynesians, with the cheerful dignity of their race; but the loneliness, the enforced simplicity, and the precariousness of life faced with the perpetual menace of the sea have made them sturdy and resourceful, and have implanted in them an abiding sense of the tragic nature of man's fate. They have both the hardihood and the enduring fear of those whose mother, the Sea, is ever at their doorsteps. None know so well the peace and beauty of her kindly moods. To none is her unescapable and mindless majesty revealed, at times, with more awe-inspiring grandeur.

Their own collective name for their half-drowned homelands is *Tuamotu:* Islands of the Distant Sea. Geographers, and the few white men who visit them, call them the Low, or Dangerous, Archipelago.

Late on an afternoon in October, a two-masted schooner entered the pass at the western end of the island of Manukura. She was a broad-beamed vessel of ninety tons, with a native crew, and the manner in which she was conned through the coral shoals within the lagoon revealed that her captain, himself a Polynesian, was no stranger to the place. The sails had been lowered at the entrance, and the ship proceeded with her engine at half-speed toward an islet that extended eastward from the passage for a distance of two miles or more. A quarter of an hour later the engine was reversed, and the vessel, losing way, was brought to anchor near the end of a ruined pier of coral slabs.

The breeze, which had become lighter with the descending sun, died away completely. Night had now fallen and the constellations of the Southern Hemisphere sparkled in a cloudless sky. In the starlight, the fringe of near-by land was a narrow ribbon of black, dividing two immensities. No sound came from the beach, nor was there any sign along the whole extent of it of human habitation. To the east and south, Manukura Lagoon seemed to stretch away to infinity, to be metamorphosed at last into sound: a faint, unceasing thunder, without beginning or end, as though somewhere, at a vast distance, the stream of Time itself were pouring over the brink of an abyss.

The vessel lay motionless; no creak of block or rudder could be heard. Two men, seated at a table on the afterdeck, their faces thrown into clear relief by the light of a lantern hanging from the boom, seemed awed and hushed by a silence so profound. They had finished dinner, and now, with their chairs pushed back, they were gazing out over the starlit water, each engaged in his own reflections. Dr. Kersaint had been medical officer of the Tuamotu Group for more than fifteen years. He was a Breton, in late middle life, short, stout and active, with a closely clipped gray beard. His bald head glimmered in the lamplight, and his blue eyes, behind gold-rimmed spectacles, were kindly and shrewd. His companion, Vernier, was a younger man, about thirty; lean, sallow of complexion, with a sensitive, rather melancholy face.

Presently the silence was shattered by the shrill complaining of blocks as one of the ship's boats was lowered from its davits, and a moment later the captain, clad only in a waistcloth, appeared within the circle of lamplight and spoke to the doctor, in the native tongue. Kersaint turned to his companion.

"They're going to Motu Tonga, across the lagoon, for a night of fishing," he said. "They will return about dawn. Would you care to join them?"

Vernier shook his head. "Not tonight, Doctor. Thank him for me, will you? I'm much too comfortable to move."

Kersaint turned to the captain and they spoke together for a moment; then the latter, with a nod to his passengers, went forward, climbed down into the boat, and took the long steering sweep, while four of his men ran out their oars. The boat moved off, shadowy in the starlight, the two men gazing after it in silence until the creaking of the oarlocks died away.

"A striking-looking fellow, this captain of ours," Vernier remarked, at length. "There must be good blood in his veins. I've been interested in the way he handles his vessel; his men, too, for that matter. They seem to know by instinct what he wants done."

"You will discover, when you know these people better, that they can converse without words, conveying their meaning in a glance, a slight movement of the head, or a lifting and lowering of the eyebrows."

"Have you known him long?"

"The captain? A good many years, now."

"Does he understand navigation? I've not seen him take a sight since we left the Marquesas."

"Oh, yes. He passed an excellent examination for his certificate. But he knows this part of the Pacific as well as the sea birds themselves. You observed how precisely he made his landfall?"

Vernier nodded. "You like these people, Doctor; that's plain," he remarked.

"I do, though I'm not blind to their failings. Five years hence you shall tell me what you think of them. I predict that, comparing them with all the races you've known, it will not be the Polynesians who suffer in the final estimate."

"Five years hence! God forbid that I should be buried here as long as that!"

Kersaint smiled. "You say that feelingly," he replied.

The cabin boy came aft to clear the table; the two men rose to resume their steamer chairs by the rail, and to light their pipes. Vernier stood for a moment, gazing toward the nearby land.

"Five years. . . ." he repeated. "I hope not. Doctor, let me speak frankly. I go where the Government sends me and try to do my duty. Thus far I have had two posts, wretched places up rivers in equatorial Africa. But I assure you that in neither of them have I had so profound a sense of loneliness and desolation as I was conscious of when approaching the land this afternoon. The sparse vegetation, the great heaps of broken coral, like bleaching bones, a few forlorn coconut palms scattered here and there . . . small wonder the place is uninhabitable. Five years among such islands? Wish me better luck, in heaven's name!"

"You have entered your new province through the back door," Kersaint replied. "Had we come from Tahiti instead of the Marquesas, we should have touched at several islands which are fairer examples of the Tuamotu. I can understand your feeling about Manukura as you see it now; yet it was once a rich island, as atolls go, and well populated. It will be peopled again when soil has had time to form."

"And when will that be?"

"Five hundred years hence, perhaps."

"A longish time to wait!"

"To a European. Down here we measure time by a different rule—in tens and scores of generations. You've heard of de Laage, perhaps?"

"De Laage? No, I don't think so."

"In his time Manukura was the seat of the administration. The Residency stood yonder, on the beach, not a quarter of a mile from where we're anchored. There was a fine church, and a flourishing village, as pretty as any in the Group."

"It seems incredible. What happened, a hurricane?"

"One of the worst that ever crossed this region."

The two men puffed at their pipes in a silence deepened rather than broken by a muffled, unceasing vibration in the air, registering on the remote background of consciousness: the sound of distant breakers thundering over miles of desolate reef. Reclining in his chair, Kersaint stared into the sky, bright with stars for which he knew only Polynesian names. Takurua was low in the east; he recognized Matariki, Tangi-Rio Aitu, and Pipiri-Ma, the Twins. They had shone on Manukura ages before human feet had pressed its sands, had stood as beacons to guide the Polynesian explorers, fifteen hundred years ago. They had witnessed the discovery and settlement of the island centuries before white men had found it, and had seen it devastated in a single night. Some day their light would again filter softly down through groves of coconut palms and glimmer on the roofs of men's dwellings where now were only bleached coral and patches of thin parched shrub. For a moment the doctor had an odd sense of existence outside of time. He turned his head.

"You are thinking that I must be a very poor doctor or a very foolish one to have remained out here fifteen years."

"Not that," Vernier protested; "but you will forgive me if I wonder how any European could be content for so long. I'm curious, I confess."

"I quite understand. The explanation is simple: I love these islands. They are barren and inhospitable, if you like, compared with the high volcanic islands to the westward, but where else is there to be found such beauty, such peace, such remoteness from the world of our times? These are advantages that appeal strongly to me. There are more than sixty inhabited islands in the Group, with a total population of about five thousand. Being the only medical officer, you will perceive that I am able to be of some use. I've had opportunities to go elsewhere, but when it came to the point of decision, I've always discovered that I wanted to stay. No doubt the authorities think me slightly mad."

"You were through the war?"

Dr. Kersaint chuckled quietly. "It's plain from that question that you agree with them."

"Don't misunderstand me, Doctor," his companion remonstrated. "It was a quite natural question."

"To be sure it was. Yes, I had passed my thirty-fifth birthday when the Armistice was signed. You must have been in your teens at that time, but no doubt you remember it as vividly as I myself."

"I recall my keen disappointment that it all ended just as I was ready to take part. What fools boys can be!"

"Men of my generation had had more than enough. The world in which our youth was passed was in ruins. We were too old to take much interest in the shaping of a new one, and still too young to fold our hands and do nothing. We had to go on living, somehow. As I look back to those days, it seems to me that what most of us wanted was merely the privilege of retiring from chaos. We could at least hope to build up something resembling order and decency in our own lives. That, certainly, was what I wished to do, and I didn't in the least care how far I might have to go in search of the opportunity. I had spent four years in base hospitals, advanced hospitals, and front-line dressing stations. By the time the war was over I had a knowledge of my trade which I hoped never to use again."

"I can well understand that."

"There was nothing, then, to prevent my ordering my life as I chose. The only near relative I had remaining was an uncle at the Ministry of Colonies. We were, naturally, drawn more closely together across the gaps made in the family circle. He was one of the kindest of men, well along in his sixties at that time, with an administrative, nonpolitical position at the Ministry. Governments rose and fell, but he remained at his post undisturbed, to instruct incoming members in their routine duties. Although he had never been out of France, he had a profound knowledge of our colonial possessions. I went to him for advice, telling him that I wanted a post as medical officer in some backwater colony as far removed as possible from Europe. My uncle was sympathetic, but he had a very delicate sense of what was fitting in his position. He would not lift a finger to help me. However, he promised that when he learned of a vacancy which he thought would suit me, he would let me know."

Dr. Kersaint broke off. "I'm sorry," he said. "I had no intention of launching out into my family history. This can interest you very little."

"On the contrary," his companion replied. "Please continue. Your uncle was as good as his word, evidently."

"Very well then . . . . Yes, he was, although he must have leaned over backward to avoid any action savoring of nepotism. A year passed and I was still waiting. At last came a laconic message, dictated, as I knew, by my uncle. I can recall the exact wording of it: 'If the doctor who wished to bury himself in the remotest of all colonies is still of the same mind, he is informed that an opportunity for interment now presents itself on the opposite side of the globe.' Under this was a note in my uncle's hand, asking me to call at ten the following morning.

"I was there on the stroke of the hour. A huge map of the Pacific hung on one wall of my uncle's bureau. He pointed out the Tuamotu Archipelago —I had never heard of it until that moment—and then proceeded to give me the bleakest possible account of conditions there. The inhabitants, he said, lived upon coconuts and fish. The islands, only a few feet above sea level, were frequently devastated by hurricanes. The few white men sent out in administrative positions were authentically buried for the period of their service. Once there, they were all but forgotten, and lost opportunities for advancement that came as a matter of course to those in more important colonies. But advancement was the least of my concerns, and the more my uncle tried to dissuade me, the more convinced I became that the Tuamotu was the post I sought. I got it almost for the asking. It seems that no one else wanted it."

"And you're quite contented? You've never regretted . . ." Vernier broke off, leaving the sentence unfinished. Dr. Kersaint rose, knocked out his pipe against the rail, and again settled himself comfortably in his chair.

"Never," he replied. "I've not had the slightest

desire to return to Europe. It's not easy to explain. You'll grant that a satisfactory life must be based on reality? Well, I find reality here."

"Reality!" exclaimed the younger man. "When we leave this place I shall find it hard to believe that the island exists at all! I scarcely know why, but even more than Africa this disquiets me, puts me on the defensive. On such crumbs of land man seems so helpless—so hopelessly, microscopically small. Tropical jungles are bad enough, but Nature typified by such an ocean . . . it is too powerful. It numbs the imagination."

"But Nature is powerful, my dear Vernier! I know: we try to forget it, and at home, where we herd together, thousands to the square mile, we very nearly succeed. But all our efforts to thwart her, to harness her, must come to nothing in the end."

"You believe, then, that our science will get us nowhere; that we shall never emancipate ourselves; that progress is an illusion, in short?"

"Progress aims at a steadily increasing security. I'm not saying that it is not a worthy end to strive toward, but think what we lose in the pursuit of it! And security is not enough; far from it! The people of these islands have been taught better. They live in the present, enjoying the simple occurrences of each day as it comes. They waste little time in planning for the future, for at any moment Nature may decide to take a hand. And they are happy, I think."

"I hope so," said Vernier with a wry smile. "Certainly, you should be a good judge of that. You must know these people as few outsiders do."

"I like them, at least, and speak their language. Situated as I am, with almost no intercourse with the outer world, one comes to take great interest in simple things: the happenings of village life, the little tragedies and comedies that develop here as well as elsewhere. In Polynesia, a doctor is a privileged person even more than at home; everyone, from the children to the great-grandparents, open their hearts to him. I divert myself by looking on, by listening to all that they tell me, until I can piece together each small drama, complete from beginning to end."

"Theirs is existence reduced to its simplest terms, I should think."

"So it is, and we Frenchmen are supposed to care little for life stripped down to the essentials. I may be eccentric in this respect, but I find it unfailingly refreshing. I am no believer in the noble savage of Jean Jacques, yet to my mind there is an elemental fineness in lives like these, free from the petty concerns that debase our lives at home. Greed, parsimony, avarice, scarcely exist among them. Thrift, which we elevate to a virtue, is a term of ridicule here. A virtue? This acquisitive storing up for the future which the peasant shares with the squirrel?"

"Have a care, Doctor!" Vernier put in with a good-humored laugh. "I shall begin to doubt you a fellow countryman."

"Don't take an elderly crank too seriously. I have changed, no doubt of it, but I fancy the war had more to do with that than the atolls."

He paused. "Are you sleepy?" he asked, presently.

"Not in the least."

"I've a mind to give you a glimpse of your new province in advance. In my mail, at Atuona, I found a letter informing me that Madame de Laage was dead. She was a remarkable woman; I had the greatest respect for her. Save myself, she was the last surviving European who played a part in a series of events in which I took deep interest. Would you care to hear the story?"

"I'd like nothing better."

"It concerns the hurricane which desolated Manukura, but bound up with that was a most unusual little drama which came under my own observation. You will understand that I didn't gather the details all at once, but before I was done, I knew everything that had happened, and, I imagine, very nearly as it occurred. The situation, like most of our troubles and perplexities, was man-made, but Nature furnished the solution in the end. Very well, then:—"

Chapter
2

This schooner was built just before the war. The people of Manukura took an almost proprietary interest in her, for her frames and knees of *tohonu* wood were cut out by them to Captain Nagle's order, and freighted, by cutter, to the shipyard at Tahiti. A remarkable wood, tohonu; it grows only on the Low Islands, and the scent of it when freshly sawn attracts butterflies for miles around. It is proof against dry rot, and grows harder and harder with age. It is twenty-one years since the *Katopua* was launched, and so far as her frames go, she is good for fifty more. At any rate, she has outlasted her skipper.

Nagle was an Englishman. He came out here in early youth, one of those unusual men who succeed in eradicating all traces of nationality. He spoke French fluently, though with a strong twang of the Midi. His compatriots supposed him an American, and Americans, an Englishman. Hearing his voice on deck, on a dark night, the natives of neighboring groups had more than once mistaken him for a Tuamotu man. His seamanship, more than his appearance or speech, proclaimed his English birth.

He began his career as cook on a brig belonging to the Maison Brander, trading to the west coast of South America, in the days when Chile dollars circulated all through this part of the world. Cook, sailor, quartermaster, mate, captain—he climbed the steps easily. He had resolved to own and operate his own vessel in the Tuamotu, and his schooner, when finally launched, represented the savings of more than twenty-five years at sea.

Like every skipper in these parts, he had a favorite island where he enjoyed a monopoly of trade, and to which he hoped to retire some day. The people of Manukura regarded Captain Nagle as one of themselves. Twice each year, with a regularity that never failed, the *Katopua* sailed into the lagoon, bringing flour, rice, tobacco, tinned beef, prints, cutlery, and other things for Tavi's store, and loading the one hundred tons of copra bagged and waiting for him in the sheds by the landing place. Nagle's memory was remarkable. He knew everyone on the island, children included: what woman was expecting a baby; which child was to be confirmed at the church; what people had relatives on other islands, and the relationship between them. He was given innumerable commissions each time he sailed, and these, no matter how small, he would execute faithfully, without profit to himself. He would match a yard of lace for a grandmother or buy a particular color of ribbon in the Papeete shops for one of the girls. In return for his many services, there was nothing within the people's power to give that Nagle might not have had for the asking.

It was natural that a Manukura crew should man the schooner. Like all Low Islanders, they made splendid seamen, once they got the hang of the ropes and compass. The best of the lot was Terangi, a lad of sixteen when Nagle took him aboard a few weeks before Germany declared war.

The men of the Tuamotu were not conscripted for service overseas, but the blood of warlike chiefs flowed in Terangi's veins, and once he had visited Tahiti and seen the drilling and departure of the troops, all the captain's influence was needed to prevent the lad from volunteering. Young as he was, he was well grown and strong beyond his years; he might have passed anywhere for eighteen or nineteen. The boy was of a type occasionally to be found among the *ariki* class: thin-lipped and aquiline in feature, and as courageous and trustworthy as he was good-natured.

Nagle had long known Terangi's mother, Mama Rua, a widow whose other children had scattered to distant islands, which is often the case in the Tuamotu, for the people are careful about inbreeding. He had had many a talk with the slender gray-haired woman and had opened his mind to her as to his hopes for Terangi. He would take the lad to sea, teach him his trade, and turn over the schooner and the business to him when he himself was ready to retire. The boy, of course, was told nothing of all this. Like others, he went to sea when he was old enough, and it struck him as natural that a portion of the ancestral land should be allotted to the captain, who would some day build a house upon it and live there.

The war years passed with only two ripples of excitement: the bombarding of Papeete by the *Scharnhorst* and *Gneisenau*, and the stir caused by Count von Luckner's raider, the *Seeadler*. Aside from these not over-serious reminders, the war might have been waged upon another planet. Copra, as you know, is a valuable source of glycerine, and the brisk demand for explosives was good business down here. The captain's views on war, which were somewhat in advance of his time, he took good care to keep to himself; but since men were fools enough to insist upon slaughtering one another, he saw no reason why George Nagle should stand aside and let others reap a harvest from a sowing which was none of his own.

When the fighting was over and the nations began to contemplate the ruins of the world they had wrecked, Nagle had built up a substantial balance at the Banque de L'Indo-Chine, and Terangi was the *Katopua's* mate.

He was twenty-one at that time: a handsome, light-skinned fellow, not tall, but already noted for his activity and strength. When the schooner touched at atolls without passes, where the boats were loaded on the outer reef, he could walk a hundred yards over the rough coral of the shallows with four sixty-kilo bags of copra on his back. Most sailors carry two; three are considered a load for a powerful man. There is no more exhausting, back-breaking work in the world than that of loading copra schooners. Terangi thrived on it, and found time between whiles to become a thorough seaman. He handled the vessel as well as the captain himself. As I have said, he was a modest fellow, without a hint of arrogance in his character, but he had a sense of dignity not to be affronted without risk. It was at this time that he got into trouble that was to have most serious results.

The *Katopua* had returned to Papeete with a load of copra, and one afternoon when the work for the day was over, Terangi, with two others of Nagle's men, was sharing a bottle of beer at

Duval's, a place near the waterfront frequented by seamen, planters, and the like. Nagle himself was there at a near-by table and saw what happened. The monthly steamer from Sydney was in port and the bar crowded with the usual customers, together with passengers from the steamer, stretching their legs ashore. Presently a paunchy, red-faced man came in and stood by the door for a moment, looking for a vacant table. He was a good deal the worse for liquor and wanted more. He had a sweaty, boozy face which he mopped with a dirty handkerchief as he glared truculently around the room, as though defying everyone in it to refuse to make a place for him. There were no chairs vacant, but he didn't mean to lower his sense of his own importance by standing up at the bar. Of a sudden he walked over to the table where Terangi and his friends were sitting and ordered them away from it. His manner said as plainly as words could have done: "I'm white. You're not. Get out!"

Polynesians are obliging and courteous folk. If the man had asked for a seat with even an approach to decency he would have had a place made for him at once. But he wanted the whole table to himself. Two of the boys got up, but Terangi didn't move. He paid no attention to the fellow and went on quietly drinking his beer. The Colonial, for so he was, was wild at being so coolly ignored, and by a "nigger" at that, as he called him. He swung his arm at full length and caught Terangi a clap on the face with his beefy paw that nearly knocked him out of his seat.

Terangi sprang to his feet and gave the fellow a blow straight from the shoulder, with the full strength of his powerful right arm, and there was no open hand at the end of it. It was precisely what the animal deserved, and there was no one present who did not think so. Unfortunately for Terangi, the man's jaw was broken. When he regained consciousness he was taken to the hospital and there proceeded to make no end of a disturbance. He was a British subject. He demanded his rights. Little as he deserved to be, it seems that he was a man of considerable authority at home—a Labourite politician or some such thing. Wireless messages passed back and forth. The British consul had, of course, been called in, and the result was that Terangi was made the victim of political expediency. He was had up for assault and battery, and despite the efforts made in his behalf by Captain Nagle and others, he was given six months in jail.

The captain was hot with anger at the result, but he took good care not to let Terangi see it. He went to visit him in the prison a few days before the schooner sailed, counseling him in a fatherly way, and urging upon him the necessity of taking his punishment quietly and cheerfully. Terangi was too strong, that was all. The next time he hit a man who imposed upon him, he must take care not to break his jaw. Six months would quickly pass. Nagle would explain matters to Marama, the young wife Terangi had married six weeks before, and deliver the little gifts the husband had purchased to take home. Terangi listened and seemed to approve of the well-meant advice, but Nagle was anything but confident of the impression he had made. Knowing the men of the Tuamotu, and Terangi in particular, he had little hope that he would submit to prison discipline.

His forebodings were soon justified. On the day the schooner sailed he learned that Terangi had gotten away the night before. The chief of police with some of his men came to search the schooner as they were about to cast off from the wharf. He was courteous and apologetic about it. It was a natural inference that Terangi might have stowed away on board, though the commissaire knew Captain Nagle well enough to be sure that he would not have connived at such business, and felt pretty certain that the boy would avoid anything that might involve Nagle with the law. After a thorough search of the Katopua he again apologized and went ashore.

That was the first of a long series of escapades. Terangi was caught within a fortnight, for he was still over-trustful of his fellow men. For centuries past there has been no love lost between the Tahitians and the Low Islanders. A pig hunter far up the Punaruu Valley made Terangi welcome in his little camp, fed him, and soon discovered who he was. The hunter invited him down to his house on the beach and betrayed him to the police while he slept. The warden at that time, a thoroughly decent fellow, let him off with fifteen days solitary confinement, the lightest of the disciplinary measures under the circumstances. And he talked to the boy like an uncle, saying precisely what Nagle had said.

Solitary confinement leaves its mark on anyone; to a man of Terangi's kind it was torture. He endured five days of it before he broke the lock of his cell and escaped to the hills once more. He was caught after a chase of several weeks, and a year was added to his sentence. His first escape had been from the road gang. Breaking jail was an offense of a different category and could not be lightly passed over. When he next escaped he took with him a military rifle from the guardhouse, with a supply of ammunition. Life in the uninhabited interior of Tahiti was not easy. He wanted a weapon for shooting wild pigs, but the authorities, of course, took a different view of his reasons. They believed that he meant to defend himself. He was becoming something of a legendary figure by this time, and now that he was known to be armed, it was easy to fancy him a desperado, a menace on the mountain trails. When he was retaken, five more years were added to his sentence.

There is no need of going into the details of his adventures during this period. It is enough to say that, during the next five years, he escaped eight times. He showed an ingenuity and a fierceness of determination in getting away that were new to the experience of the police. He could be kept in prison only by methods too inhumane to be practised steadily, and the authorities bore in mind the trivial nature of the offense that had brought him there in the first place. Vain attempts were made to cow him by threats. As soon as he was given a measure of freedom within the walls, he would find a means of getting outside them. The Tahitians, although they betrayed him time after time, had a secret admiration for him, and he became a hero to every small boy on the island. The gendarmes who were compelled to hunt him in wild and difficult country saw him in a different light, as did those higher up. He was making a laughing-stock of authority. Meanwhile, he had accumulated a total sentence of sixteen years.

Although he felt keenly the injustice of his first imprisonment, he was too much of a man to hoard up bitterness. He knew that his captors were doing no more than their duty and nursed no resentment toward them. But he had to be free, whatever the cost.

On each of Captain Nagle's infrequent visits to Tahiti, he had gone at once to the jail in the hope of seeing Terangi; but what with escapes to the mountains and the fact that visitors were not permitted to see those in solitary confinement, three years passed without his having so much as a glimpse of the prisoner. Meanwhile, a new warden had arrived from France, one of those just men, as coldly impersonal as the Law itself. At last, more than four years after the affair in Duval's bar, Nagle learned, at the wharf, that Terangi, after his latest escape, was once more in custody. Nagle went straight to the Governor, over the warden's head, and was granted permission to see him.

His reception at the prison, under these circumstances, was a chilly one. It was clear from the warden's manner that there was to be no more nonsense about this Terangi matter; no more making a mock of authority. He took the Governor's note, glanced at it, bowed coldly, and led the way to Terangi's cell. There was a new iron-studded door of hardwood, four inches thick, equipped with a formidable series of locks.

The cell was about eight feet square and lighted by a single small window, high in the wall. Terangi was tethered by one leg, the chain attached to his ankle, shackled to a heavy ringbolt set into the floor of stone. He had altered little, outwardly, save that he was now a man, fully matured, but Nagle was conscious of a profound inward change. All the joy of life had gone out of him, and there was a sombre look in his eyes. Nagle scarcely trusted himself to speak; he took Terangi's hand and held it between his own. The warden stood in the doorway, looking on.

If Terangi was moved, he showed no sign of it. He had himself well in hand. When the silence was broken, he asked for news of his wife and mother, and of the little daughter he had never seen. Nagle pulled himself together and contrived to answer with some show of cheerfulness, but he was soon aware that Terangi was as eager to close the interview as the warden himself. Nagle left the prison in a gloomy frame of mind.

There was a stir on Tahiti when Terangi escaped once more. It happened about three months after Nagle's visit. The new warden had been oversanguine about breaking Terangi's spirit. He kept him in solitary confinement until he seemed thoroughly subdued, and then gave him tastes of liberty when traps were laid: apparent chances to escape which the prisoner was too wary to take advantage of. At last he was permitted to have his hour of exercise without shackles, in the prison yard.

He was enjoying his brief walk up and down the yard late one afternoon when the road gang was brought in. There were two guards inside and two others came in with the prisoners. The gate-keeper had unlocked the heavy door and the last of the prisoners had been checked in when Terangi made his dash. For a moment the guards were numb with astonishment, and five seconds leeway was all that Terangi required. The man at the gate jerked out his revolver and fired as Terangi seized his wrist. The others were coming on the run, afraid to shoot. A heavy blow over the heart knocked the gatekeeper out, and before another shot could be fired, Terangi was outside.

Papeete cemetery lies in a valley on the opposite side of the road a little beyond the prison. He sprinted among the gravestones with half a dozen men in chase, firing as they ran, plunged into the bush at one side of the valley, and was gone. It was a most sensational escape, in broad daylight, but this final break was accompanied by tragedy. When they picked up the gateman he was dead; it seems that he had a weak heart. Once again, Terangi had struck too hard.

Capturing him, after his repeated escapes in the past, had become a kind of grim sport to the police, a game they played with ever-increasing skill, and they had no doubt that they would soon have him in their hands again. Tahiti, as you may know, is made up of a large peninsula and a small one, connected by the low narrow isthmus of Taravao. They hunted him like a hare on Tahiti-Nui, raising the villages with offers of reward. As a matter of policy, for the benefit of the native population, the government let its intentions with respect to the fugitive be known. As soon as he was caught, he was to be sent to the penal colony at Cayenne, in French Guiana, and there would be no more escaping for Terangi, ever.

Keen-eyed men were posted on the ridges, the valleys were scoured by boar hunters with their dogs, and on one occasion, at long range across the valley of Vairaharaha, he bounded through the fern in plain view for more than a hundred yards, under a heavy fire. Slowly and relentlessly he was hunted from one refuge to another and driven toward the Taravao Isthmus. There they made certain of taking him, and a large posse of trackers was stationed to seize him when he attempted to cross to the smaller peninsula. But once more he eluded them. Choosing a black, rainy night, he managed to slip through the chain of pursuers to conceal himself among the wooded ridges and untrodden peaks beyond Teahaupoo, the wildest, most inaccessible region of all Tahiti. But he could flee no farther. He was hemmed in on three sides by the sea, and approaching from the northwest came a small army of pursuers led by the police. It was a hard search but a thorough one; no coign of the rocks was left unexplored. The net was drawn closer and closer, but when at last it was closed at the extremity of the island, the quarry was not in it. Terangi had vanished as though he had melted into the mists that hang over those wild and gloomy mountains. No one had seen him nor had a sign of him been found.

Chapter
3

There were four European residents on Manukura at this time: de Laage, the Administrator, and his wife; Father Paul, and myself. The first, in point of length of residence, was Father Paul. He had come out to the Tuamotu as a youth fresh from the seminary and had spent more than fifty years in the Group without ever having returned to France. He was one of those transparently good old men, so often found in the service of the Roman Catholic Church, whose obscure and devoted lives the world never hears of, but which mean so much to the little flocks they serve. He came from peasant stock in a mountain village near the Spanish border, and his education had been strictly clerical. In his childhood he had been taught to believe in all sorts of ghosts and devils. He found hierarchies of these awaiting him on Manukura, where the natives were nothing if not superstitious. They were very close to being heathen in those days; in fact, they had never before had a missionary stationed amongst them. Father Paul met this situation in a characteristic way. He developed a curious sort of worship, Christian, to be sure, but with a generous mixture of paganism in it. This had nothing to do with basic doctrines, of course. Those he held fast to and taught his people to do the same. They had the deepest love and veneration for him, and he was worthy of it. He accepted the teachings of the Church with the unquestioning simplicity of a child. It is common, in our day, to speak slightingly of these devoted souls. Bigots they may be, in the sense of adhering to one system of belief and excluding all others; but their lives will not suffer in comparison with those of men who believe in nothing, not even in themselves. The world does well to make room for its Father Pauls.

His church, which he had planned and built, largely with his own hands, stood midway in the village. There had gone into it the simplicity of his own nature and the beauty inherent in his faith. It was a coral-lime structure, capable of holding the entire population of one hundred and fifty, with narrow Gothic windows and a little bell tower, all so perfectly proportioned that I doubt whether the best ecclesiastical architect in Europe would have found anything to criticize. It was truly astonishing that an old peasant priest should have worked with such rightness of instinct.

Although in his late seventies, he had the vigor of a man much younger. He had never been ill in his life; with his duties—he was spiritual guide to the natives of half a dozen islands—he had no time to be. His courage, which was as remarkable as his industry, came in part, no doubt, from radiant, unfailing health, but it was based upon his absolute trust in God. Of the six islands under his charge, the nearest, Amanu, was fifty miles away; the farthest, Puka Puka, lay at a distance of more than one hundred and fifty. His only means of visiting his widely scattered parishioners was a small half-decked cutter. She was a stoutly built, sea-worthy boat, but when I tell you that she was only sixteen feet over all, with a five-foot beam, you will understand that it required hardihood to make long voyages in so tiny a craft. Low Islanders are thorough seamen and anything but timid folk, but even they shook their heads over what they considered the father's recklessness. His only companion on these voyages was a fourteen-year-old lad, Mako, one of the sons of Tavi, the storekeeper, who trusted in him as implicitly as the priest trusted in God. They would set out in all kinds of weather and be absent, often, for a month or six weeks together. In the course of time the natives became convinced that the priest was, indeed, an instrument in Divine hands. Nothing could harm him or those under his protection.

One afternoon in March—this was in 1925—the priest and Mako were returning to Manukura from the island of Hao, which lies about seventy-five miles to the southwest. They had left Hao the afternoon before and were still some thirty miles from home. Their galley was a tin-lined box filled with sand which they kept on their half deck in good weather. Mako had prepared supper, after which the father had lain down for an hour or two of sleep.

Mako sat at the tiller humming softly to himself, keeping an eye on the compass and scanning the horizon from time to time. Now and then he would catch glimpses of noddy terns, alone, or in flocks of half a dozen or more, flying landward from their day's fishing far offshore. They were Manukura terns and would be alighting on Motu Atea or Motu Tonga in an hour's time. With a breeze so light, the father and he could scarcely hope to reach the pass before dawn. Nevertheless, they were moving. The little cutter was sensitive to the faintest breath of air.

The sun had set and the sea was bright with the blurred reflections of fluffy, fair-weather clouds, glimmering softly in the afterglow. Glancing off to the left, Mako's attention was attracted by a black object floating on the surface of the water, half a mile or more off the course the cutter was following. At that distance it looked scarcely larger than a match stick and would not have been remarked by one less keen-sighted than a Polynesian boy. Mako kept his eye turned steadily in that direction. Now he would lose sight of it for a moment; then it would reappear riding over the long smooth undulations of the sleeping sea; then he would lose it once more. There was something curious in its appearance; it seemed to rest a little too high in the water for a bit of water-soaked wood made heavier still with barnacles. There was a projection, an excrescence of some sort; if the object was a tree, it might be the fragment of a limb broken off close to the trunk. Of a sudden the lad's eyes widened in astonishment. He bent his head and peered under the deck where Father Paul was stretched out on a thin mattress, asleep.

"Father! Father Paul!"

The old priest stirred and raised his head. "Yes; what is it, my son?"

"There's something off to leeward! Come quickly, Father!"

Aroused by the boy's manner, the priest crawled back to the cockpit and stood gazing in the direction Mako indicated. Dusk was gathering rapidly and in the half-light a moment or two passed before he made out the object.

"You have sharp eyes, my lad. I see it now. What is it, a log?"

"No, Father."

"*Eaha nei!* What, then?"

"A canoe, capsized. I think there's a man clinging to it."

"A man? Impossible!"

"I saw him move; I'm certain of it. He lifted his arm."

Quickly the priest took the tiller while Mako slacked away a little on the sheet. They bore down directly on the object.

"Lad, so it is!" the priest exclaimed, incredulously. "He sees us, I think! Stand by, now, to grasp his arm!"

Both stared ahead, scarcely believing the evidence of their eyes. The canoe floated bottom up. The outrigger was gone and the man clinging to the hull was half sitting, half lying astride of it. In the dusk they could make out little save that he was bareheaded and all but naked. The priest hailed him when they were within a few yards, but there was no reply. The cutter was brought into the wind directly alongside. Mako was a strong lad. He seized the man's outstretched arm as he slid off the canoe and drew him to the cutter's side; then, seeing that he was too far spent even to cling to the gunwale, he leaned far over and dragged him into the cockpit.

Leaving the tiller, Father Paul was on his knees beside him at once. For the next half hour they worked over him, giving him coconut water, a few swallows at a time. He was in a pitiable condition from thirst and exhaustion. His hair was long and matted and his cheeks covered with beard. It was not until Mako lit the lantern that the man was recognized. It was Terangi. He had been picked up at a spot—if one may speak of a spot in mid-ocean—nearly six hundred miles from Tahiti. That distance he had covered in a small outrigger canoe such as the natives use for fishing inside their lagoons. If I have failed, thus far, to give you an adequate conception of Terangi's character, this simple statement of fact will suffice.

He was utterly spent, and presently, without once having spoken, he fell into a heavy sleep. Between them, they managed to push him under the shelter of the deck. Mako remained squatting beside him throughout the night while the priest sat at the tiller. Shortly after sunrise, the boy climbed the mast and caught sight of the palms on Motu Atea, the islet that curves around the eastern end of Manukura lagoon, twenty miles distant from the village islet. It was barely within view; the blurred irregular line of the highest trees could just be seen breaking the line of the horizon. The priest then ordered Mako to lower and furl the sails.

They waited, the cutter drifting, throughout the morning. The day was far spent when Terangi awoke. Mako prepared food for him and he ate ravenously, saying little this while. Father Paul's one indulgence was his pipe, a meerschaum with a quaintly carved bowl at the end of a long stem. It held a full ounce of tobacco. He lit this while Terangi was at his meal, watching with deep concern and quietly waiting for the man to speak. Mako attended to his wants with an air of awestruck devotion, almost with the reverence with which he assisted Father Paul at Mass. If Terangi was a hero to the boys of Tahiti, you can imagine what his fame was among those of his own island. They had long since heard, of course, of his many escapes and his encounters with the police. Mako, having been the means of saving his life, had a heart filled with happiness. To sit near him, to serve him, to be noticed by him, were privileges so great that he could have found no words with which to express his gratitude. No more than the priest had he recovered from his astonishment of the night before, but he had the ingrained courtesy of his race. It was Terangi's privilege to satisfy their curiosity or to refrain from speaking, as he chose.

When he had finished his meal, the lad rolled a cigarette for him. The man smoked as he had eaten, in silence, with keen enjoyment. Then he turned to the priest.

"Life is good, Father," he said. "I little believed, last night, that I should see the sun of another day."

The priest nodded. "It was Mako who spied you."

Without turning his head, Terangi laid a hand on the boy's knee. "I saw you at a distance of two miles—three, perhaps. I feared that you would pass to windward of me on the course you followed. I could do nothing; my strength was gone. Two days and a night I had been clinging to the canoe. The outrigger was badly damaged. I had tied it together as well as I could; then I was again capsized in a heavy squall. There was no repairing the outrigger that time. I could do nothing but wait for the end."

"*Nofea mai oé?*"

"From Tahiti."

"You have come from Tahiti? Alone? In that tiny canoe?"

"Yes, Father."

"Terangi *Tané!*" Mako exclaimed softly. All the lad's capacity for wonder, awe, devoted love, was implicit in the exclamation.

"I came by Mehetia, Anaa, Haraiki, Reitoru, Tahéré. I had no compass. I steered by the sun and the stars. I made a little sail of copra sacking. It is six weeks since I left Tahiti. No one has seen me at any island. I landed on the *motu* far from the village islets. When the weather favored, I went on again. It has been a weary time."

That is as much as Terangi ever told of his voyage, as remarkable an exploit, I dare say, as one man has ever accomplished in such a tiny, unseaworthy craft. Mehetia, his first island, is about sixty miles from the nearest coast of Tahiti. Anaa, the second, is two hundred miles farther on, and Haraiki the same distance beyond Anaa. Luck was with him, of course, until his final misfortune, and Terangi was too good a seaman to take unnecessary chances, but one needs vastly more than luck to make such a passage as that. Polynesians are still great historians, and Terangi's voyage is known now, both in song and in story from one end of Oceania to the other. It is worthy to pass into the legends of the race.

But to get on with the story— He did not speak again for some time, but sat with his hands clasped loosely, staring at the deck beneath his feet. The old priest gazed at him compassionately, observing the gaunt face, the eyes terribly inflamed by sea water, but more than this, the sombre indomitable expression within them.

"Where are we, Father?" he asked, presently.

The priest pointed to the north. "Manukura is there, just over the horizon."

"And you are waiting here for . . . ?"

"For you. For night, if you would have it so."

"I escaped from prison three months ago. You knew, on Manukura?"

The priest shook his head. "We have had no news since the *Katopua* last came. She is expected again soon."

Terangi was again long silent. At length the priest laid a hand on his shoulder. "My son," he said, "I first saw you an hour after your birth. I watched you grow from babyhood to manhood. All the events of your life have been open to me. You trust me?"

"I do, Father. Wait before you speak further. When I escaped this last time, a guard of the prison was killed."

"By you?"

"Yes. He was at the gate of the prison yard. The gate was open to let the prisoners enter who had been working on the roads. It was a chance. I rushed at the guard. He fired a pistol at me and missed. I struck him on the chest, with my fist. Who would believe that such a blow could kill? But so it was. The man was dead when they took him up. This I learned when hiding in the mountains."

"You were innocent of the wish to kill him?"

"As innocent as I am of the wish to kill Mako. The man had befriended me more than once. I wished only to escape."

"It is a grievous sin, but with God, the intent is all. He can forgive heavier ones in those who truly repent."

"But that will not give life to a murdered man, and so it will be judged by those who sent me to prison. If I am caught, I shall be sent to a place they call Cayenne. Where it is I do not know, except that it is far away. And those who are sent there never come back."

"Terangi . . ."

"Yes, Father?"

"No one knows that you have left Tahiti?"

"No one save you and Mako; that is certain. They must be searching the mountains for me still; but it may be suspected, by this time, that I have escaped elsewhere."

"What would you do now?"

"I would see my wife once more, and my mother, and the child that I have never seen. Then let what will come. The little daughter is mine?"

"Can you doubt it?"

"I have been eager to believe it. There has been no one else, then?"

"Never! Your wife has thought of no one but you."

"Six years is a long time, and she is young. I could understand if . . ."

The priest interrupted him sternly. "Never, I tell you! You do her an injustice to hold such a thought!"

"I wished only to make sure."

"You do not know your wife."

"And what time have I had to know her? We were but six weeks married when I was put into the prison."

Father Paul's stern expression softened to one of compassion. He had no struggle with his conscience in deciding what his attitude toward the fugitive should be. Secular law was one thing, Divine law another. He had nothing to do with the first, everything to do with the second, and he believed, as did everyone else on Manukura, except the Administrator, that Terangi was a deeply wronged man. Secular law could be implacably, inhumanly just. So it had been in Terangi's case, but he well knew that de Laage took a different

{ 34 }

view of the matter. The father had little hope that
the Administrator could be kept long in ignorance
of Terangi's presence on the island. In a place
where everything was known, and quickly known,
concealment would be enormously difficult. There
was no man or woman on the island who would not
guard the secret as carefully as himself, but the
children in their innocence might easily betray
him. To avoid this possibility it would be best
that none should know save Terangi's nearest relatives: his wife and mother; Fakahau, the chief, his
father-in-law; and Fakahau's brother, Tavi. The
priest was careful to impress upon Terangi the
great need for caution.

"I have been a hunted man too long to be blind
to the danger," he replied. "I shall be taken again,
that is certain; but I shall have some weeks, even
months, perhaps, before they learn where I have
hidden. The Administrator is now on Manukura?"

"No; but he is expected to return with the Katopua. He has been visiting the islands to the
south."

They then proceeded to discuss plans for the
immediate future, and it was decided that Terangi
should conceal himself on Motu Tonga, an uninhabited islet eight miles across the lagoon from
the settlement. Father Paul would inform only
those mentioned of Terangi's arrival; the family
could then take counsel as to what was best to
be done. Sail was now gotten on the cutter. A little
before sunset they raised the land, but night had
long since fallen before they were coasting along
the lonely reefs of Motu Tonga. Mako ransacked
the scanty supplies on board, preparing a little
bundle of things for Terangi's immediate needs: a
waterproof tin containing matches and tobacco, a
pareu, a bed quilt, a clasp knife, various other ar-

ticles. These he rolled into a tight bundle covered
with a piece of matting, and Terangi fastened it
with a cord, high on his shoulders. The priest
steered the cutter to within a few hundred yards
of the reef. Great combers were breaking across it,
but Low Island folk are as much at home in the
surf as the fish themselves, and a night and day of
rest had restored Terangi's strength. When they
had run midway along the islet he shook hands
with his rescuers, slipped over the cutter's side,
and was soon lost to view, but they waited until
they heard a distant halloo from the beach. The
cutter then stood off to the northeast, and at
dawn entered the pass by the village islet.

Chapter
4

You will agree that chance had played a sorry trick upon those two young people. I am speaking of Terangi and his wife. Father Paul had told the barest truth in assuring Terangi of Marama's loyalty. She was sixteen at the time of their marriage, and all through the years of his imprisonment she had lived for the day when she would have him at home again. As year followed year and the Manukura folk learned of the appalling sentence he had piled up by his repeated attempts to escape, most of them gave up all hope of his return, but not Marama. She gloried in his unconquerable spirit and loved and respected him the more for what some of the older people called his stubborn foolishness. Other young men would have liked nothing better than to take the absent husband's place, but none of them dared tell her so. However, when it became known that Terangi had sixteen years to serve, several hesitant offers were made to Marama. They were refused with vigorous scorn.

She came, as did Terangi, from the best blood of the Archipelago. For all the chaotic social conditions that followed the European conquest of Polynesia, pride of birth was not lost amongst its people. It was not an empty pride; in ancient times the best men *were* the best men, and that is true to-day. Fakahau, Marama's father, was first on Manukura because he was the natural leader of his people, as his father and grandfather had been before him. The office of chief, under French rule, is elective, but the business of choosing one on Manukura was a mere formality. It would have been unthinkable that anyone except Fakahau could have been chosen. It is curious to reflect upon the antiquity of some of these Low Island families. That of the chief traced its descent back through more than forty generations. Terangi, too, was of the *ariki* class; his family was second in distinction only to that of Marama.

She was a handsome girl, the elder of Fakahua's two daughters. Her skin was a light olive and her rippling, copper-colored hair framed the oval of her face to perfection. You observe that I speak of her with a certain enthusiasm. During my years out here, traveling from island to island, I have had time to become a connoisseur, middle-aged and heart-free, let me add, in types of Polynesian beauty. I have yet to find a girl worthy to be compared with Marama.

Tita, her little daughter, was six years old at this time. I have spoken of the unkindness of chance in separating the young parents so soon after their marriage. This was more than made up to them in the manner in which the family was reunited. Father Paul was not able to inform Marama of Terangi's return. As it happened, she had gone to Motu Tonga two or three days earlier, and was there when Terangi swam ashore.

Motu Tonga was the wildest and loneliest of the lands on Manukura reef. No copra was produced on this islet, which was left in its natural state. Its coconut palms were self-sown, growing as nature would have them among thickets of *purau* and the screw pine. The undergrowth was, in most parts, sparse and scattered: vines and hardy, shrublike trees found what nourishment they could in the coral sand, but toward the centre of the islet were several magnificent *tou* and *pukatea* trees, huge in size and centuries old, that had been growing there in heathen times. Motu Tonga had been the site of the ancient settlement, but after European discovery and with the coming of the trade in copra and pearl shell, the village had been moved to the more accessible islet by the pass.

Marama had gone, with Tita, to gather a particular kind of snail shell found in the coral sand of Motu Tonga. The work of gathering these shells would have been considered tedious by most women; but those of Manukura, having leisure in abundance, loved the occupation, and from these almost microscopic shells, of various colors, they made beautiful *hei,* the shell wreaths worn by atoll folk on their pandanus hats, both as a decoration and to keep them from blowing away on windy days. They sometimes went in parties on these excursions, half a dozen women together. They would take food and bedding with them, build little shelters of fronds to sleep under, and divide their time between fishing and shell gathering. It was a distraction in their lives, of which they never tired. As often as not they would go alone, or with some of their children, as Marama had done on this occasion.

She and her daughter suited that lonely landscape. They gave it significance; the sea birds themselves were not more at home in it than those two. I like to think of them there, as they were on the day of Terangi's arrival. Marama was in complete ignorance of his presence, of course; they had long been asleep when he swam in through the breakers, nor had they seen Father Paul's cutter at dawn the following morning. It was Tita who discovered her father. Marama was preparing their breakfast over a fire on the outer beach and Tita had wandered off by herself along the shallows of the reef to the westward. Presently she came running back, too excited for speech; not frightened, but in a child's state of hushed astonishment when it sees something it can't account for. After some questioning the mother learned that what had been seen was a man, asleep not far from their camp.

"But who, Tita?"

"I don't know," the child replied.

"You must know! Is it Rongo? Or Maviri? Or Tamatoa?"

Tita shook her head at each of these suggestions. "It's no one," she said. "Just a man, an ugly man."

Marama was puzzled by the child's replies no less than by her manner. In a settlement so small as Manukura, everyone is known; no child of six would have been at a loss to name any man or woman in it.

"You saw his face?" she then asked.

Tita nodded. "It is covered with hair, like Father Paul's. I could see only a little. Then I ran away."

The mother, who had been kneeling by the fire, rose to her feet. "Come, show me where he is," she said. Taking Tita's hand, she crossed the long slope of the outer beach and followed it westward for several hundred yards. Presently the child drew back. "He's there," she whispered, pointing to a clump of bushes a little distance before them. "Don't go, Mother! Perhaps it's a *varua ino!*"

A century of contact with Europe has done little to lessen native superstition; they still believe in spirits, both good and bad. An evil spirit is known as a *varua ino*. Father Paul believed in them as implicitly as did the natives themselves, but he had taught them that a good Catholic need have no fears in their presence. To make the sign of the Cross was to draw a charmed circle about one which no evil spirit could pass. The mother now did this and Tita the same. The child clung tightly to her hand as they moved soundlessly toward the screen of bush and peered through it. Terangi was stretched out on the sand, asleep, just beyond. He was lying on his side, his face turned toward them. Marama recognized him at once.

I leave you to imagine her astonishment and joy, but she didn't cry out or try to waken him. Somehow, Terangi had come home. She didn't question herself as to how this miracle had taken place, although she scanned the beach for the sight of a canoe. He was sleeping like the dead, the gaunt face covered with beard, the hollow eyes deep in their sockets, told her all that she needed to know of the sufferings he had gone through. Laying a finger on Tita's lips, she seated herself with the child in her lap, where they could look at him. Tita's curiosity was, naturally, great, and she could see from the expression on her mother's face that there was nothing to fear.

"Who is it?" she whispered.

"Your father, Tita. He has wanted to come home all these years, ever since you were a tiny baby. I have told you that, often."

"I know; and the wicked men on Tahiti wouldn't let him."

"But now at last he has come."

"Who brought him? Did he come alone?"

"Hush! I don't know. He is very tired. We mustn't disturb him. He will tell us when he wakes up."

The sun was well above the horizon by this time, and at first the low bush shaded him. Before the light could strike his face, Marama gathered an armful of pandanus leaves and quickly plaited them, making a little screen which she propped up at his side to shelter him. Tita became restless. Her father was a mere name to her and she was evidently disappointed at this first view of him. She was glad when her mother sent her off to play along the beach.

It was midmorning when Terangi stirred and opened his eyes. Marama was sitting beside him, facing him. He stared at her vacantly; then he sat up, scarcely believing her presence. She was not a large woman, anything but the Amazonian type. On the contrary, she was what might have been called petite in figure, but now she got to her knees and gathered him in as a mother might have done, holding his head against her shoulder. She was too profoundly stirred for tears and clung to him with a combined fierceness and tenderness, as though he were a child rather than a man—a child who had come to her for protection. She was bare-footed, bare-legged, dressed in the simple island fashion, in a flowered *pareu* fastened across her breast and reaching to her knees, and her hair fell loosely over her arms and shoulders. Terangi was naked save for a pair of ragged dungarees, chopped off at the knee, in which he had swum ashore.

Neither of them could find words, at first. Terangi put back her hair and held her face lightly between his hands, gazing into it as though he would never have done. Then he found his voice.

"Marama, we are here, we two. I must speak the words to make sure, after so many years."

"We three," she replied.

"*Eaha?*"

"We three," and she pointed to where Tita was wading through the salt-water pools a hundred yards distant. She called to the child, who came running toward them and halted at a little distance, gazing solemnly at her father, with curious, appraising eyes. After a little urging she consented to sit in his lap and he stroked her dark hair and felt her sturdy arms and legs as though trying to convince himself of her reality.

They remained there for half an hour or longer, too happy for much talk, but making tentative efforts now and then to build bridges of words across the abyss of time, nearly six years deep, that had separated them. Tita helped. Despite her father's beard and his forlorn, unkempt appearance, her feeling of strangeness and disapproval soon vanished, and she prattled away as though he had always been with them.

Marama got quickly to her feet. "How hungry you must be! I have half a dozen fine *tinga-tinga* which I caught early this morning, and a tin of beef, and rice and hard biscuits from Tavi's store. I was ready to cook our breakfast when Tita came to tell me a very ugly man was asleep on the beach here."

Words soon came easily to both. They talked like two children, interrupting one another, as they returned to Marama's camp. Her hut was a lean-to such as fishermen make for shelter on the uninhabited islets, open toward the sea, which was ruffled to the deepest blue by the fresh southeast wind. Some coconut husks were smouldering in front of the hut.

Marama gathered up a handful of leaves and dry sticks and placed them on the coals. Terangi fetched water from a small well, three or four feet deep. In the Low Islands, there are such shallow wells on most of the large *motu*, and they are used, chiefly, for washing clothes. The water is brackish at the bottom, but, after a rainfall, quite fresh on top. Marama tasted it. "Only a little salt," she said. "It will do well for the rice." An iron pot was hung over the fire and, while the water was heating, she broiled the fish on the coals beneath. Terangi climbed a near-by palm and threw down a dozen green drinking nuts. When the rice was cooked, Marama emptied into the pot a tin of beef that had been opened and left to simmer at the edge of the fire. She stirred the savory mess well so that the juices and the rich gravy of the meat should be thoroughly mixed with the rice.

Terangi sniffed the fragrant steam. "How good it smells!" he said. But for all their hunger, when the meal was ready they set it aside to cool, having the native dislike for hot food. When they began, they ate slowly, with keen relish, talking little until the needs of the body had been satisfied. The meal was a ritual with them, as it is with most people where food in any variety is scarce. They know the pleasure of anticipation and the sharp delight of eating.

Marama gave him the news concerning their families and of the changes that had taken place during the years he had been absent: who had died, who married, what children had been born, and their names. Terangi then told her of his voyage, passing over it as briefly as he had in telling Father Paul, and how he had been picked up by the priest and Mako. Marama questioned him eagerly concerning the details, but soon gave over, seeing how unwilling he was to speak of that weary time. He said little of Tahiti and his experiences there, nor did he speak of the future. Like other men of his race, he had the precious faculty of recognizing present happiness and the wisdom to seize upon it, without forethought or afterthought. Women, whatever the race, are more practical; nevertheless, Marama said nothing of plans throughout the day. It was not until late that evening that she brought these matters forward. Tita was asleep, and they were lying on a mat, under the stars.

"We must speak of what is to be done," she said. "You have a plan, perhaps?"

Terangi was long in replying; then he said: "I have come home. I have you and Tita, and I shall see my mother once more. I shall stay as long as I can . . ."

"And then, what?"

"You know as well as I," he replied, sombrely. "They will find me."

She sat up, taking his hand and holding it fiercely between her own. "Find you? Never! Believe that as I do! Believe it for Tita's sake if not for mine!"

Terangi shook his head. "I shall not blind myself to what will come. I shall be taken again. Soon or late they will come here. I know them too well."

The hopelessness in his voice chilled the girl's heart. She caught a glimpse, through his eyes, of an inexorable thing called the Law, from which there was no escape. To her, it assumed the shape of Monsieur de Laage: cold, courteous, impersonal. She shuddered inwardly at the thought of the glance of those blue eyes which saw so much, which seemed to read one's very heart. She feared that, strive as she might, her manner would betray Terangi's presence to the Administrator. One thing was certain: she must avoid meeting him, face to face, for as long as she could.

"What of this, Terangi?" she asked, presently. "The *Katopua* is coming soon. Captain Nagle will go south this voyage and east as far as Mangareva. We three could hide in the hold before she sails. The sailors are all Manukura boys. The captain could put us ashore at one of the unpeopled islands: Tematangi, or Maria, perhaps."

"He must not be told."

"Why not? He would help us. You are like a son to him. My own father could not have been kinder to me than he has been all the years you have been away."

"Think of the danger to him. He is a man of importance and well thought of by those at the seat of government. If it became known, great trouble would come to him. We must not call on him for help. He would give it gladly, to his own hurt."

"It need never be known."

"You deceive yourself, Marama. And even on Tematangi or Maria we would not be safe for long. Vessels sometimes call at those islands for firewood or to fish. They would be certain to find us. The sailors on most of the schooners are men from Tahiti. They are treacherous people and would like nothing better than to betray me. Every time I have been caught, a Tahiti man has told the police where I was hiding. There is a reward of five thousand francs for him who betrays me again. I saw the notice posted on a tree in Tautira." He broke off again and was silent for some time. "Let us speak no more of this," he added. "We have this little time together. Let us not spoil it by thinking of what is to come."

They were in the midst of this conversation when they were startled by a low hail such as the natives use when approaching others unnoticed. Terangi sprang to his feet, but there was no time for concealment, nor was there need for it. The man was within a dozen yards of them. It was Fakahau, the chief, and with him Mama Rua, Terangi's mother.

She was a slender woman of sixty, with thick white hair which she wore in a single braid down her back. She was as resolute in character as her son, but the gentleness, the wistfulness, of age was in her face. Terangi was her only son, and all the love of her heart was centered upon him. The deep anxiety and grief she had suffered during his imprisonment had aged her beyond her years, but while she felt keenly the wrong that had been done him and the cruelty of his prolonged punishment, her spirit had been neither crushed nor embittered by it.

Marama ran forward to meet her; then she walked aside with her father, leaving Terangi alone with his mother for a while. Presently they rejoined them. A stranger, looking on at the meeting, would not have guessed its significance. Tuamotu folk, particularly the men, are not demonstrative at moments when their deepest emotions are engaged. Fakahau's pride in his son-in-law was as boundless as his admiration for his courage and resourcefulness, and Terangi, ever since his father's death, had looked upon the chief in the light of a parent; but the two men greeted one another as casually as though they had last met only the day before. Mama Rua clung to her son for a time, her head on his shoulder. Then she drew back, brushing away her tears.

"Enough, my son," she said. "It has done me

good to weep a little. Now we must talk. We have
little time. We must return to the settlement at
dawn. Marama, you and Tita are to come with
us."

"To-morrow, at dawn!" Marama exclaimed.

Her father spoke. "You can stay no longer now.
The reason is plain. There must be no suspicion
of Terangi's presence here."

"But such a thing will not be thought of," Terangi replied.

"Even if it were, there is no man or woman on
Manukura who would not shield him as eagerly as
ourselves," Marama put in. "They would bite their
tongues out rather than betray Terangi."

Her father nodded. "It is true," he said, "but
think how much safer and better it will be if none
save ourselves know."

"That is impossible," Marama replied. "Such a
secret cannot be kept. Others are certain to learn
of it."

"If Terangi were to stay on Manukura it would
be impossible. Elsewhere he may be safe. You
shall go with him, you and Tita."

Terangi looked up quickly. "Go? Where?" he
asked.

"Listen well, Terangi," said the chief. "This plan
we three have made: your mother, Tavi, and I.
No time is to be lost, for the *Katopua* has been
expected this week past. The Administrator will
come back with her. You should be gone before he
arrives. It is your freedom alone that matters. If
the wind favors, you must go the moment our
preparations can be made."

"But where?"

"To Fenua Ino."

"To Fenua Ino? We three, alone?" Marama
asked, in dismay.

"You would not wish to be left behind?" Mama Rua asked quietly.

"Never!" the girl replied. "Where Terangi goes, I go, but I had not thought of Fenua Ino. It is no more than a name of ill-omen to me. What Manukura man has seen it except from the sea? Who has ever set foot upon it?"

"Terangi's grandfather has, and my father, and I with them," Fakahau replied. "I was young, then, no older than you are now. It is not an evil place for all its name, and only eighty miles from here. Some old trouble happened there, so long ago that neither my father nor my father's father knew what it was. But this I know: some of our people lived there in times long past. Then the island was abandoned; they came to Manukura, bringing the bones of their dead, save those of one man who was my ancestor. The land was made forbidden, and so it has remained through all the years."

"I have passed the place a dozen times on the *Katopua*," Terangi remarked, "but none of us ever landed there. Captain Nagle told me that he himself has never done so. There are two small *motu* on the reef and nothing more. The rest is bare coral washed over by the sea, mile after mile after mile. There is said to be an islet in the center of the lagoon, but no such land is shown on the chart. If it exists, it lies at too great a distance to be seen from the reef."

"The land exists, and you shall go to it," said Fakahau. "It was there the people lived in the ancient days. It was there I went with my father and your grandfather; they wished to bring home the bones of our ancestor who had been left behind. My father knew where he had been buried and we found him."

{ 49 }

"How great is the land?" Terangi asked.

"A score of families might live on it. It is good land, higher than any of the motu of Manukura. There is a narrow crooked passage through the reef on the northern side; a canoe can be taken inside, but no schooner could pass. The lagoon is full of shoals for a distance of a mile or more; then you have deep water to the islet, which lies almost in the centre of the lagoon. On a calm day it is a three hours' paddle from the nearest point on the reef."

Marama and Terangi listened with intense interest. The girl's eyes shone with a new light; as for Terangi, he was another man. He said nothing, now, of waiting for what must come.

"The very place!" he exclaimed.

"No white man has ever been told of the islet," said Fakahau. "Once you are safely there, you can live with your mind at peace. You will never be found. You need have no fear of the place. The ancient tapu had never been removed, but this was done by my father at the time of our visit."

"Why, then, was it never made known?" Marama asked.

"My father and Terangi's grandfather had their reasons, no doubt. Perhaps they thought it best that the land should remain a forbidden place in the eyes of all our people. I will not say," he added, gravely, "that they may not have been given foreknowledge of the need there would be for a refuge there for one of our family, in years to come. So, at least, it has happened. We may well be grateful to them for their silence."

"A lonely place," Terangi said, musingly. "We should see no one from year's end to year's end. For that I am prepared. But Marama and Tita . . ."

"Lonely? We three together?" Marama replied.

"Have no fears. We shall be happy where you are."

"You could not come with us, Mother?" Terangi asked, hesitatingly. "But no," he added quickly. "We should not think of it. The life would be too hard at your age."

His mother made no reply for some time, except to take his hand, stroking it gently. "It is what I would wish," she said, "but it is not to be. . . . Terangi, I knew that you were coming home, though I did not speak of it to Marama. I wished her happiness to be unlooked for, and so it was. Your father came to me in a dream, twenty-six nights ago. There is no doubting what the dead tell us; least of all, such a man as your father. He told me that I should see you here, on Motu Tonga. A little time only, and for the last time."

"And what more?"

"He told me that I should be with him soon, very soon. It is true. I know it. I feel it," she added quietly.

Her two children, son and daughter-in-law, listened, awestruck and profoundly moved. Low Island folk believe as implicitly in certain kinds of dreams as Europeans believe in what appears before their open eyes. Who am I to say that such belief is absurd, the foolish credulity common to primitive folk? I have seen too many of their dream prophecies fulfilled not to have, to say the least, an open mind in these matters. They know, as we do, that some dreams are mere nonsense, without significance; but when their loved dead appear and speak to them, telling them what is to come, there is no doubt in their minds as to the truth of what they are told. If they remember their words and are convinced, upon awaking, that no mistake has been made in recalling them, they act upon them with the same quiet assurance with which we accept any of the certainties of life. So it was with Mama Rua in this instance. She believed in her approaching death no less firmly than she had believed in Terangi's homecoming, and her listeners believed with her. Fakahau had already been told of the dream, and his confirmation only added to the certainty of the revelation as it affected the others.

They were silent for some time, each of them engaged in his own reflections. Marama was the first to speak again.

"You have yet to say, Father, how Tita and I are to go with Terangi. How can our absence be explained?"

"This too we have thought of. It is a hard thing. . . . We can see but one way. It must be believed that you and Tita have been drowned."

"Drowned . . . !"

'This can be arranged so that none shall suspect. When all is ready, you and Tita shall come again to Motu Tonga. A reason for the return can easily be found. Two or three days later, when I know that you three have gone, I shall send here after you. Some of your clothing shall be found and the canoe in which you came, in such a way that all shall believe."

"Truly believe? Our own people?" Marama asked.

"They must, at first," Mama Rua replied. "Our kinsmen alone shall know the truth; it must be disclosed to no one else. Later, perhaps, others may be told, but not now; not until some years have passed. For Terangi's safety, nothing must be known, lest some careless word should betray him. Even now I could wish that Mako did not know. Good lad that he is, there is danger. He is too young to be trusted with such a secret."

"You have told Father Paul of this plan?" Terangi asked.

"No," said Fakahau. "He would not wish to be told, of that I am sure. It is best for the father's sake that we keep him clear, from this time on, of any knowledge of what we do. He will suspect, but will be saved from the burden of knowing. For the same reasons, Captain Nagle shall not be told."

"We shall need many things on Fenua Ino," said Terangi.

"You shall go in my great canoe," said Fakahau, "which I will suppose has gone adrift and out the pass. Tavi is now preparing the things you will most need. There will be room for a good store of food and supplies: tools, canvas, rope, pots and pans, clothing, bedding—nothing shall be forgotten; you can depend upon us to see to that. At some future time I shall find means to visit you, never fear."

"When must we go?" asked Marama.

"You and the child must return here the day after tomorrow, in a small canoe. The village should witness your departure, thinking that you come again for shell gathering. That night the large sailing canoe will be loaded and ready and Mako will sail it across. For your sakes I dare not come again. The canoe is too heavy to draw across the reef and launch through the breakers. You must go out through the passage after the moon has set. I need not tell Terangi to keep as far as possible to the westward in approaching the pass. If on that night the wind should not favor, you must wait here until it does."

"Short is the time we have together," said Marama, sadly. "I am thinking of you, Mother, and Terangi. This one night and no more."

Mama Rua took the girl's hand. "My child, it must be so," she said. "If I could have my way you would be gone before the new day comes."

Chapter
5

Fakahau had not been mistaken in urging the need for haste. Not that he considered the immediate danger serious; but he wished to have Terangi safely away from Manukura before the Administrator's return. This was not to be, however. The *Katopua* was sighted the following morning.

The coming of Captain Nagle's schooner was the great event in island life. I used to catch something of the excitement myself. For at least a week before she was expected, every youngster on the island would be on the lookout for her. They would post themselves on the tops of the tallest coconut palms along the outer beaches and remain there for hours, each one eager to give the first shrill hail: *"Te pahi! Te pahi!"* that would be taken up from mouth to mouth and quickly passed along the entire length of the settlement. On that day all work was suspended. The women would get into their best finery and the men don their Sunday suits of white drill, and long before the schooner appeared in the pass, everyone on the island would be assembled at the landing place. The vessel brought bags of mail from distant relatives and friends, and the *parau-api*—the news. The members of her crew, from Captain Nagle to the cabin boy, well understood what was expected of them. They gathered the details of every event, no matter how trifling, that happened in the island world, and knew how to make the most of their stories. The events of the greater world beyond aroused only a feeble interest on Manukura. What the people wanted most to hear was about old Paki of Fakarava, who had married a gay young wife; about the Hikueru man who found a pearl worth fifty thousand francs; about the woman of Marokau whose arm had been bitten off by a shark; about Terangi's latest escape. These topics of conversation, elaborated in the most meticulous detail, were made to last a full six months.

The *Katopua* carried to the world's markets all the copra that the island produced, and everything consumed there—save coconuts and fish—was fetched in her capacious hold. Food, clothing, building materials, tools of every sort, the very tree cotton that filled the mattresses on which the people slept, came from Tahiti. The Manukurans could live—had lived for centuries—with none of these things, but copra made them rich, and what they earned, they spent. Some of the elders used to find it wearisome to exhaust their credits at Tavi's store, but the young men and women had no such difficulty. The day after the schooner came, there would be shelves filled with gay new prints, tins of beef and salmon and fruit; behind the counters were barrels of flour, cases of tea, coffee, tobacco, rice, and, in the long showcases, cutlery and jewelry of all sorts: knives, scissors, flash lamps, brooches, rings, and ear pendants of nine-karat gold. Stocks were usually low by the time of the schooner's next visit, but when Tavi was sold out, as had happened more than once in the past, his clients returned to the simple life of their ancestors in a care-free manner which proved how little, at bottom, important luxuries meant to them.

The return of the Administrator made this latest arrival of the *Katopua* an event of more than usual importance. Fakahau was in the forefront of the crowd, wearing the tri-color sash of his office, with his brother, Tavi, beside him, and Madame de Laage on his right hand. De Laage had been absent for three months, and as the vessel was threading her way through the shoals we could see him with his binoculars leveled upon his wife. The moment they were alongside, he stepped over the rail and greeted her in his usual courteous, smiling manner. His pleasures and his duties were performed with the same unalterable respect for decorum; he was not the man to make a public display of his more intimate feelings. After a word or two with Madame de Laage, he turned to the chief. I could see how surprised he was not to find Father Paul present. He liked all the events of life to fall into their customary places, and Father Paul's absence on schooner day was, indeed, extraordinary; such a thing had not happened within memory. Nevertheless, de Laage proceeded as usual, shaking hands and chatting for a moment with Fakahau, Tavi, and myself, then standing with Madame de Laage while all the men and women of the island came forward to welcome him home. This ceremony concluded, he retired to the Residency.

It may be well, at this point, to give you a clearer picture of de Laage. He was a tall, spare man, with prominent blue eyes, a bald spot at the crown of his head, and a large, straw-colored moustache. There was Flemish blood in him. In temperament he resembled the English rather than the French type of administrator. He believed in the *mission civilatrice*, in education on European lines for the natives, in the necessity for maintaining white prestige. A devout Roman Catholic and a Royalist under the skin, he regarded science as a kind of heresy, liberal thinking with aversion, and politics as a game for the vulgar. He was not ambitious. The fact that he had remained in the Tuamotu for eighteen years—a post extremely distasteful to him —sufficiently indicates that he was not moved by a desire to get on in life, and no doubt the authorities at home were glad to have so dependable a man in the position. He was guided by another motive than the wish to rise: a sense of duty, lofty, stern, and rigid; it dominated every act of his life. As for his integrity, no man, white or native, had ever questioned it.

His reading was confined almost entirely to *L'Action Française*, to which he was the only subscriber in this part of the world. Immense bundles of the little Royalist daily reached him twice a year when the schooner came in. These he arranged in order of dates, and each morning, when he sat down to his fruit, eggs, and coffee, he opened "to-day's" newspaper, then anywhere between six and eight months old. The shelf in his office contained all the books he possessed: a few volumes of law, manuals for the guidance of officials, and one arid-looking tome on the Science of Administration, which was a kind of Bible for him.

In a place like this, successful administration consists in stopping trouble before it starts, and the official must know, above all, what is going on. He is the judge of the land court, for one thing, and since there is a good deal of litigation about land, the titles to which are based upon genealogy, it is essential to have some idea of the rights of each case in advance. The best administrator, in

a way, is the best listener, and the native—even
the exceptional man who knows a little French—
will speak his thoughts only in his own tongue. To
work with an interpreter is to learn only what the
interpreter desires one to learn. After his eighteen years in the Group, de Laage did not know
eighteen words of the language—at any rate, he
was never heard to pronounce them. The truth is
that he was a born *chef de bureau*. Without his
wife, he could never have made a success of his
job.

When he went to the war, in 1914, Madame de
Laage remained on Manukura. Officially, there was
no Administrator; actually, she carried out her
husband's duties so capably that the islands have
never been better governed. Only a handful of
white men have mastered the language of the
Tuamotu: an ancient, beautiful, highly inflected
speech, capable of infinite shades of meaning. Madame de Laage spoke it fluently, with a lack of
accent that was positively startling when one
glanced at the speaker. Small enough to be called
doll-like, with a gift for dress that always made
her fresh and charming, even on a cutter voyage,
she looked like a girl in her twenties until one saw
her face. Even then one would hardly have
guessed her age within ten years. The tropical
sun seemed powerless to harm her complexion;
she preserved her fresh coloring well into middle
life, but it was her eyes that first attracted attention. They were dark, almost black, and alight
with intelligence and interest in the world.

Most women in her position would have expired
of loneliness and ennui, but her life, I am sure,
was truly happy. I doubt whether she was ever
bored with her own companionship; she had too
many resources within herself for that. She was

an excellent musician and never tired of her piano, which she herself kept in tune. Unlike her husband, she was a great reader, and the books in their library were all hers. A sister in Paris kept her supplied with post-war fiction, drama, biography, and the like, but her tastes were not confined to general literature. She had a fine collection of works on Polynesia, from the eighteenth-century volumes of exploration to modern treatises on anthropology, botany, on the fish in the lagoons and the shells to be picked up along the reefs.

In character, the man and wife were as unlike as the books each read. In his honest, straightforward way, de Laage looked up to his superiors and down on those he considered beneath him. Madame de Laage looked neither up nor down, regarding all men and women as fellow human beings, interesting and worthy of respect. She could go into any house on Manukura and spend an agreeable evening with the women, joining in their tasks and taking part in discussions of village affairs as though she had been born on the island. She could weave a hat or a pandanus mat with the best of them, or design and sew one of the native patchwork quilts. She never wearied of exploring the minds of her companions, for the differences of outlook which usually act as barriers between races were to her no barriers at all. I am sure that she looked forward without pleasure to the day when her husband would be transferred to another field, or, failing that, be pensioned off at last to return to France.

She was his superior in many respects, and must have been aware of the fact. I believe that she was genuinely fond of him; it may have been because he had such need of her. Certainly, there was no question of his love. He was a lonely man, intensely reserved; all the warmth of his nature was centered upon his wife. When away from her he suffered tortures of anxiety. I have made voyages with him when my heart went out to him on this account. Not that he made a show of his concern, but knowing him as I did, I also knew how utterly lost and miserable he felt when absent from home.

It was their custom, on the day the schooner came, to have Father Paul, Captain Nagle, and myself to dinner with them. I went with the captain that evening, rather earlier than usual. Madame de Laage appeared in the doorway to receive us, and a moment later her husband stepped out on the verandah in the mess jacket to which he never failed to change for dinner. He informed us that Father Paul had sent word asking to be excused.

"It's extraordinary!" he added. "I've never known him to miss one of our dinners in all the years we have been here. And he was not at the wharf this morning. Have you seen him, Doctor? He's not ill?"

I replied that I had seen him at work in his garden early in the afternoon.

"I'm profoundly glad that he is not to come this evening," Madame de Laage said, feelingly. "Eugene, have you told them the news?"

The Administrator sighed. "I have not wanted to think of it," he said. "I have spared Captain Nagle thus far, but you will both have to share it with us, soon or late. I may as well tell you at once. It is this: in the bag of mail you brought for me from Tahiti, Captain, I found a letter from the Bishop. He has set me a task . . . a task, he frankly admits, that he has no heart for. In a word, Father Paul's Order has recalled him to France."

Madame de Laage turned to me. "Think of it, Dr. Kersaint! What stupidity! What injustice to uproot Father Paul after all these years! It will kill him! I know it! What can Monseigneur be thinking of to consent to such a cruel thing!"

"It is not a question of consent on the Bishop's part," de Laage replied. "He realizes as we all do what this will cost Father Paul. You must know how the religious Orders are administered. The discipline is almost military; commands from headquarters must be obeyed without discussion. The Bishop tells me that he wrote a four-page letter to Father Paul, attempting to soften the shock, and then tore it up. He has passed on to me the task of delivering these harsh orders with whatever words of comfort I can summon."

Captain Nagle was as shocked as myself at the news. As for Madame de Laage, she could scarcely keep back the tears as we spoke of it. She perceived much more vividly than her husband the full cruelty of the situation. For more than fifty years, Manukura and the half-dozen neighboring islands had been Father Paul's world. Never in all that time had he even gone so far afield as Tahiti. No man could have lived a happier, more useful life. Now he was to be deprived of his church, his garden, of his work in which all his heart was centered, and of his last well-earned pleasure which he regarded with serene anticipation: being laid to rest, by his children, as he called them, in the coral sand of the island he loved.

"But why should they want him in Paris?" Madame de Laage asked. "He shan't go! We mustn't let him go! Eugene, don't let him know! There must be a way to prevent such an unkind plan from being carried out."

"I have no doubt they have excellent reasons for wishing his return," her husband replied. "What possible justification would I have for

failing to deliver to Father Paul the commands of
his Order? He would not thank me for such mistaken officiousness in his behalf. No; much as he
will hate to go, he is a soldier of the Church. His
duty is to obey."

Madame de Laage was silent for a moment. "It
is true," she replied, wretchedly. "He will have
to be told, but don't let it be at once. Captain, you
mean to call again here before returning to Tahiti?"

"Yes," said Nagle; "I am going to Mangareva
this voyage. I shall be back at Manukura in a
month's time."

"Then wait, Eugene, until the *Katopua* returns
before telling Father Paul! This will give him one
more month of happiness."

"Nothing is to be gained by putting off unpleasant tasks," her husband replied. "The Bishop
asked me to let the father know at my earliest
convenience."

"Please, for my sake," his wife urged. "The delay won't matter in the least, since he can't go in
any case until the schooner returns."

She pleaded with him so earnestly that the Administrator consented to the delay, but it was
plain that he was disturbed about it.

A moment later Arai came to announce that
dinner was on the table. She was a girl of sixteen, a younger daughter of Fakahau, and lived
at the Residency in a relationship peculiar to
Polynesia: half servant, half companion and
friend to Madame de Laage. For all their pride of
birth, Polynesians are the most democratic of
people. No tasks are considered menial, and a
chief's daughter could serve at the Administrator's table without any loss of dignity or prestige.
I learned long afterward that Arai knew of Ter-

angi's return; in fact, all the immediate members of the two families had been informed, but there was nothing in her manner on this evening that could have betrayed the presence of the secret she shared.

It was natural that our talk, during the course of the meal, should have drifted to Terangi's latest escape. The whole island was, of course, discussing it; I had heard but little else throughout the day. The Administrator informed us that he had received a communication on the subject from the Governor of Tahiti.

"Terangi has been playing the very devil there," he announced gravely. "He has become a thoroughly dangerous and intractable prisoner and the authorities are determined to capture him. I am aware, Captain Nagle, that he was once your protégé. It may be that the question is an unfair one, nevertheless, I shall ask it. Do you think there is a chance of his making his way here?"

I have no doubt that Nagle thought, secretly, that there was an excellent chance, but he was not to be caught off his guard.

"You don't believe, Monsieur de Laage, that he would compromise me by stowing away on my ship?" he asked, smiling.

"Never!" Madame de Laage put in warmly. "I know him too well to suspect that."

"I am certain that he would never do it with your consent," de Laage replied, "but I can't share your belief in this young man's delicacy of feeling. Your sailors are all Manukura boys. They would gladly conceal him aboard, if they could do so without your knowledge."

"The police on Tahiti share your belief," Nagle replied, drily. "They made a thorough search of my ship before we left Papeete. It isn't the first time by any means. They even examined my large sea chest and the drawers under my bunk."

"Don't imagine for a moment that I suspect that you would connive at the business. You would do me a great injustice if you supposed that. I am thinking of the natives of the Tuamotu. They would shield him on any of the atolls. Granted that he could not hide in the *Katopua,* it strikes me that he might work his way out here little by little, traveling from island to island in cutters or sailing canoes. He would certainly attempt this if it were at all possible."

Captain Nagle shook his head. "He would have come long since if there had been any chance of it," he replied.

I observed that Arai, who was serving the fish course, was listening with all her ears. Madame de Laage gave her husband a glance that missed its mark, for he went on:—

"The Governor wrote to put me on my guard. It's astonishing where Terangi can have got to. He escaped more than three months ago and Tahiti has been searched from end to end without result. Not only Tahiti: all of the other islands of the Society Group have been thoroughly combed without a trace of the man being found. The police believe that he has somehow gotten clear of the Archipelago. They suspect that he is already somewhere in the Tuamotu and that Manukura is his goal. They've had more than enough of this incorrigible fellow. He has made a mock of all lawful authority. I thoroughly agree with them. Such things can't be permitted. Cayenne is the only place for such characters. The Governor informs me that he is to be sent there when he is taken again."

An awkward pause followed. De Laage realized of a sudden that his zeal had led him to say more than he should have in Captain Nagle's presence. He took advantage of the silence to fill the glasses once more, and we were soon speaking of other matters.

Chapter
6

Manakura village was deep in the profound slumber of the hours before the dawn. The booming of the breakers along the outer reef, now loud, now muted in the flaws of the light breeze, thundered an unceasing accompaniment to the people's dreams, a sound of which they would only have become aware had it ceased. High among the fronds of the palms, noddy terns perched with their young, croaking with long-drawn, muffled tones. Here and there, behind the outdoor kitchens, swine grunted softly, rooting in the soft coral sand for left-overs from the evening meal. A flock of curlews, on their annual flight to their Arctic breeding grounds in Asia or North America, passed overhead with lonely piping cries. Presently, far off at the eastern end of the islet, a rooster crowed, and cock after cock took up the challenging call. The colony of maina birds roosting in the purau tree behind the de Laages' dwelling wakened all at once and burst into a chorus of whistles and twitterings. Slowly the gray light from beyond the horizon gave place to the flush of dawn.

In two houses of the settlement there had been little sleep that night. Both the chief and his brother, Tavi, had been busy with the preparations for Terangi's departure. There had been need for the greatest secrecy in this matter, and the work of collecting the supplies had taken place in the small hours of the morning; they were stored, well concealed, in the canoe shed belonging to Fakahau. All the preparations were now completed. It remained only to wait for another night, when Mako would sail the great canoe to Motu Tonga. By the dawn of the third day, Terangi, Marama, and their daughter would be out at sea, their canoe well below the circle of Manukura's horizons.

For all his sleepless night, Tavi was at his place behind the counter of his store at the usual time. Trade was always brisk after the *Katopua's* arrival, and for an hour or two in the early morning it was as much as Tavi and his older children could do to take care of the eager press of customers. Tavi was a huge man, like Fakahau, with thick black hair lightly sprinkled with gray. He was a true cosmopolitan, having left Manukura in boyhood. He had spent many years at sea and there were few large ports, the world over, that he had not visited; but he had returned home at last to marry a Manukura woman, well content with what he had seen and learned of the ways of other peoples. He was a man of fine intelligence, a shrewd observer, and could have missed little, during his roving life, worthy of attention. I used to spend evenings without number in Tavi's company. A more amusing and interesting companion would have been difficult to find.

No man on the island took a greater interest in Terangi, or had been so thoroughly pleased to learn of his many escapes from prison and the ceaseless trouble he had given to the police of Tahiti. He was as proud of his niece's husband as though he had been a blood relative, and Fakahau himself was not more determined that he should never again fall into the hands of authority. On this morning, when the press of business for the day was over, Tavi set out along the village street in the direction of the cemetery.

The houses of Manukura were scattered for a mile or more along a single wide roadway that followed the curve of the lagoon beach. There was not a prettier village in the whole of the Archipelago, nor one in which the inhabitants took greater pride. They kept it scrupulously clean; fallen fronds and leaves were carefully swept up and burned each day, and owing to the sparseness of the undergrowth, one had a series of charming views. The Residency stood at the far western end of the village, near the passage into the lagoon. It stood in its own grounds a hundred yards from its nearest neighbor. Tavi's store and dwelling, a low square building of wood, with a verandah in front, faced the lagoon beach near the coral pier where the schooner was moored. Some little distance farther to the east was the chief's house, and across the road from it the little thatched home of Mama Rua. Beyond this again was a depression in the land which crossed the islet from north to south. It had been made, evidently, by some great storm in the past, and as the ground was moist and swampy there, a footbridge had been erected over it. On the opposite side stood the church, and here another path branched northward to the cemetery.

Manukura's dead slept in a lonely plot of ground by the outer beach, three hundred yards distant from the church. The place had been a sacred one long before Commodore Byron's discovery of the island, for the temple of the old god, Tangaroa, stood there, and three ancient *pukatea* trees near by had been planted in his honor. No trace remained of the heathen temple; its stones were now incorporated in the walls of the church, but something of the ancient atmosphere of sacredness seemed still to linger in the air, as if the heathen god's presence were tolerated by the God of Father Paul.

The fringing reef was little more than a stone's throw distant, where, all day long, the smoke of the breakers drifted away to leeward, shot through with rainbow lights, half veiling the surf when the swell was high. Save for the old trees and the greenish gloom beneath them, the burying ground was all white: the coral sand, the low wall that surrounded it, the blossoms of the flowering shrubs, the headstones of the dead—even the ghost terns that sailed back and forth like tiny voiceless spirits were as white as snow. No sound of life in the village reached this place. In the cool of the early morning or evening, husbands or wives or mothers would come to spend an hour beside some grave, deriving pleasure from a sense of the physical closeness of those they loved. Despite the thunderous silence and something eerie in the air, Manukura cemetery was not an unhappy place.

Here it was that Tavi found Fakahau standing with Mama Rua at her family burial plot, directing the labors of two young men. They had finished digging a grave and were now erecting above it a little roof, supported on four posts, to keep out the sun and rain. Close by, sheltered with a roof of corrugated iron, long since red with rust, was the tomb of Mama Rua's husband. The headstone was a slab of white washed cement, inscribed: "Nui Matokia, 1868-1919." The headstone of another grave was so weathered that the inscription was barely decipherable: "Terangi Matokia, 1881." Terangi's grandfather lay here, born in pagan times when no man knew his age. Three or four women were buried in the same plot, as well as two children who had died in the influenza epidemic of 1918.

Tavi joined the little group in silence, looking on as the chief directed the work of the two young men. A European unacquainted with Polynesians would have found something fantastic in the scene, had he known the circumstances, but none of those present considered it in that light, nor did the rest of the Manukura folk. All knew by this time that the spirit of Mama Rua's husband had appeared to her in a dream, telling her of the imminence of her death, and they no more doubted that the prophecy would be fulfilled than they doubted the rising of tomorrow's sun. It was fitting that the members of her family should proceed at once to make ready her last resing place.

"Let the posts be painted white," Mama Rua was saying; "and it is time that the roof over my husband's grave was changed. You will see to this, Fakahau?"

The chief nodded as he laid a hand on the old woman's shoulder. "Come and sit in the shade, Mama. The sun grows over-warm."

"Nui has waited long for you, Mama," said Tavi. "Can he not wait a little longer?"

She shook her head as they walked slowly to the nearest tree and seated themselves there, out of hearing of the men at work on the grave. "No," she said; "I have seen my boy as I was told that I should. My time is at hand. I would see him once more, if I could," she added wistfully. "It is hard, having so little time with him after all these years. A few hours—no more! I must be content with that."

"Shall we wait another day?" Tavi suggested. "I could send a small canoe tonight, to fetch him over. You could meet him at the far end of the islet when all are sleeping."

The old woman shook her head. "The risk would be too great," she replied, firmly. "They must go to-night, as we have planned. . . . Fakahau, I should like the singing to be at your house."

"It shall be done," said the chief. "Where is Marama? She has Tita with her?"

"She will not let the child out of her sight. There will be little danger on that account. It is your son I fear, Tavi. Mako has the secret in his eyes."

"I have cautioned him well," said Tavi. "He is not to leave the house this day."

"Coffee! Was that on the list?" Mama Rua asked, abruptly, after a moment of silence.

"Yes," said Tavi. "Nothing has been forgotten, Mama. Set your mind at rest. The coffee is with the other things, well packed in a small cask."

"There is room and to spare in the big canoe," said Fakahau. "Every tool they will need can be taken. Sugar, rice, flour—they will not lack even such things for many months."

Mama Rua sat with her hands clasped lightly in her lap, gazing to the north across the great empty desert of the sea. She sighed and shook her head. "It is a hard choice for them," she said. "I am thinking of your daughter rather than my son. A lonely life it will be for her and Tita."

"My daughter's place is with her husband," said Fakahau. "We must not grieve for them. They are young and strong. They have their child, and others will come."

"One thing you have not thought of, Tavi," said Mama Rua. "Let Marama's frigate bird be taken with them. When it returns we shall know that they have arrived safely."

"Aye, that will be well," said Tavi. "I will catch it when I return to the village."

They broke off their talk as they observed Madame de Laage approaching. The chief stood up to greet her. She seated herself beside Mama Rua, who took her hand between her own, stroking it gently. For all her years on Manukura and her knowledge of its inhabitants, Madame de Laage had never been able to accustom herself to the native attitude toward death. The realization that Terangi's mother, bright and active for her years, had decided to die and was supervising the preparation of her own grave inspired in her an emotion bordering upon horror. She had seen others, old men and women, apparently in the best of health, do the same. The sudden cessation of the will to live, and the calm acceptance of what they believed was their fate, were incomprehensible to a European. Strangest of all, there was nothing morbid in the native character; certainly, despite the teachings of Christianity, their thoughts were never shadowed by the problem of evil, nor by reflections concerning the cruelty and the futility of life. Mama Rua wanted to be with her husband, that was all. Now that he had called her, she would go, and willingly.

"You have your husband," she said, as she continued stroking Madame de Laage's hand. "Should he go before you, you will understand."

Her old friend's gentle voice and the touch of her hand brought a sudden dimness to Madame de Laage's eyes. "Aye, Mama," she replied, softly; "*tei iaoé*. You know what is best. Perhaps I understand, a little."

She then spoke quietly of other matters with these old friends, but soon rose to go, perceiving

with her woman's intuition that they wished to
be alone. As she walked slowly back along the
path to the church, a realization came to her of the
immense remoteness of her life from that she had
known as a girl, in Europe. What would her sister
in Paris think of such a scene as that she had just
witnessed? How fantastic life would seem to her
in these scattered island worlds! But not more so
than the islands themselves, minute ringed shoals,
microscopic in size, compared with the vast ocean
round about.

She halted before Father Paul's small coral-
lime house which stood not far from the church,
built against the wall that surrounded his garden.
The door to his little reception room stood open;
there was no one within. She went on to the gate
leading into the garden and looked in.

Madame de Laage loved this place, as indeed
we all did. The garden was a truly remarkable one
to be found on a low island. The work of creat-
ing it had been a labor of love with Father Paul
over nearly half a century. Tropical fruits and
flowers common to the high islands will not grow
on the atolls unless planted in high-island earth.
Little by little, with extraordinary patience, zeal,
and skill, the father had fashioned a little paradise,
two acres in extent, sheltered from the sea winds
by a wall eight feet high. Captain Nagle had had
his share in the work; he never came to Manukura
without bringing the priest two or three tons of
rich volcanic earth, in copra bags, from Tahiti or
the Marquesas. Mixed with humus and coral sand,
this made the best of soils. It was like entering
another world to pass from Manukura in its natural state into Father Paul's garden. He was a born
horticulturist. His breadfruit, lime, and orange trees
were as fine as any to be seen on the high islands.

He had laid out paths, shaded with banana and papaia trees, flower beds, small lawns, and arbors covered with flowering vines whose fragrance had never before perfumed the air of a low island. There was nothing throughout the Archipelago to be compared with this garden, and it was typical of its creator that its fruits were reserved for his parishioners: the children, the old, the sick. His reward, and he found it ample, had been the joy of making it, and continued to be the joy of improving it.

Madame de Laage found him hard at work there, his rusty old *soutane* tucked up under its cord, helping as well as overseeing some boys who were mixing a heap of rich reddish soil with decayed coconut husks and coral sand, preparatory to filling a five-foot hole that had been dug near the wall.

"Here you find me, my child," he said, looking up at her approach. "See what a fine cargo of earth Captain Nagle has brought me. I am planting a young avocado on this spot. I have never yet tried one on Manukura."

"It is certain to thrive, Father, under your care," Madame de Laage replied.

"Let us hope so. If it does as well as this mango, I shall be well content. Have you seen finer fruit than these on Tahiti?" He pointed to a basket containing half a dozen fruit, on a bench near by. "They are for Tavi's daughter, she who will soon have her child. Will you take them to her on your way home? But keep one for yourself."

"She shall have all. There could be no kinder gift. Women's appetites are fickle at such a time. You are always thinking of others, Father."

"Nonsense! I have had more pleasure in growing them than she or you could have in eating them.

Come, sit you down, my daughter. My old bones are stiff; I need rest. You look sad, or do I imagine this? You have had no bad news in your letters from France?"

"I have come from the cemetery," Madame de Laage replied. "Mama Rua is there, with Fakahau. Her grave is ready. Will she die, Father?"

"But it is certain," the priest replied, quietly. "You have seen it happen with our old people before."

"I know; but it is so strange, so unnecessary, so . . ."

"So unnatural, you would say. I do not think so. What is natural is not only what we Europeans know. I have lived on Manukura too long to believe that."

"But she is so full of life. I can't believe it possible that we are to lose her."

"She knows, and she will go as she says. The thought of death troubles you now. It will not be so when you are old like Mama Rua and me. I too have my grave ready." He smiled as he pointed with the stem of his long pipe to a shady corner of his garden where, in fact, Father Paul's own grave had long since been made. "You see? I am a true native; I ought to be, after so many years. Like the others, I wish to be prepared. But I shall not go soon. No, no! Not for many years. I shall live to be one hundred. And I could wish to live one hundred more!"

"You have no desire to go home again?"

"Home?"

"To France. To see our dear country once more."

The old man shook his head, quietly. "What should I do there, my child? I should die of homesickness at home, as you call it. No; the wish of my heart is to close my life here where I have labored for fifty-five years. But what a talk of graves and dying we have had! And here is my fine young avocado tree to plant!"

The Administrator had spent all of that day at his desk. Over the large, immaculate table where he worked hung a portrait in oils of his father, a veteran of the Franco-Prussian War, in the uniform of a colonel of infantry. The old gentleman, who bore a striking likeness to his son, stood with a hand on his sword, the upper part of the figure in sharp relief against a curtain of velvet, looped back to give a glimpse of a smoke-dimmed battle scene. De Laage had commanded a battalion of the same regiment in 1918, and on the opposite wall his own photograph in his major's uniform faced the portrait painted in a more romantic age. There was only one other picture in the room: a double-page in color from *L'Illustration*, in a narrow frame of dark wood. It was entitled, "The Café de la Paix in War Time," and imparted to me, at least, the very breath and spirit of those stirring days. It was one of those hazy, autumn afternoons at the hour just before the lights began to twinkle on the streets. The *kiosque* of a news vendor was in the foreground, with the crowded pavement and the famous terrace beyond, where soldiers of all the Allied armies were sipping their drinks at the little tables.

Whether or not this picture aroused any emotion in de Laage, I can't say. I never heard him speak of it. In his office his mind was, I think, wholly engrossed in his work. He took deep pleasure in making his reports, worded in polished, academic French, and written without a blemish in his fine, regular hand. His returns on vital statistics, on the imports and exports of the Archipelago, on trans-

fers of land and the proceedings of the various
land courts over which he presided, were posi-
tive works of art. He may have known that the
fate of these masterpieces was but transitory: to
be glanced at by some clerk who would jot down
a hasty notation before consigning them to the
central archives. If so, the thought was not permitted to interfere with the satisfaction he derived
in composing them. His office was a refuge from
disturbing reflections of whatever kind. When he
closed the door and glanced about him at the rows
of manuals on their shelves, his letterpresses, the
chairs for visitors aligned along one wall, the files
where at a moment's notice he could lay his hand
upon any one of a thousand papers, and the inexhaustible supply of official forms and writing materials stowed away in drawers for each size and
kind, he felt the pleasure of a creator contemplat-
ing the small ordered world he has made.

Outside of his office, unoccupied with routine
tasks, he was less sure of himself. There were de-
cisions to be made, judgments to be given on matters still in their fluid state, that had not yet solidi-
fied for comfortable handling in reports of things
past and done with. The Bishop's letter concerning
Father Paul was such a matter. Neither he nor
his wife referred to it again, either at dinner or
later during their evening on the verandah, where
he smoked his cheroot while she played through
the new music she had received from France. Nevertheless, the conviction that he had been remiss
in his duty worried him profoundly. He should
have informed Father Paul at once, as the Bishop
had requested, but he had promised his wife to
withhold the news until the *Katopua* returned.
His word to her would have to be kept.

He retired at ten, slept badly for an hour or two,

and found himself wide-awake once more, still thinking of Father Paul. Liking and respecting the priest as he did, every day of delay would make the task of telling him the harder, and he was deeply grieved, as much upon his wife's account as upon his own, at thought of the change that would be brought into the life of their little community by the departure of the priest. Who would be sent to replace him? One thing was certain: whoever came, he could never fill the place of Father Paul.

Endeavoring to dismiss these unpleasant thoughts from his mind, he fell to thinking of Terangi and what the Governor had written concerning him. Was it possible that the fellow might find his way back to Manukura? He would try, certainly. All of his people were here. Nagle was a thoroughly honest man. It wasn't likely that Terangi could succeed in stowing away on his schooner, but all the Tuamotu people were making a hero of him; a cutter would be placed at his disposal at any island of the Group. It would be a simple matter to land a solitary passenger on one of the remote Manukura islets and sail away, leaving no one the wiser. Compounding a felony meant nothing to these people where one of their own race was concerned. It was bad, this lack of respect for the law, due, no doubt, to slackness in administration. De Laage tossed restlessly in his bed, wondering whether he himself were not in part responsible for the native attitude toward authority. Had he been too easy-going in his own administrative policies? That, certainly, had been the case on Tahiti with respect to the enforcement of police and prison regulations. Terangi's numerous escapes, apparently at will, offered convincing proof of the fact. Justice should be well tempered with firmness in dealing with the inhabitants of all these islands. They were only too ready to take advantage of what they considered weakness on the part of the authorities.

De Laage consulted his watch by the light of his flash lamp. It was past one o'clock. He rose, dressed, stepped out on the verandah, and then proceeded along the path that led by the outer beach, away from the village. It was a beautiful night, cool and cloudless. He hoped that a three-mile walk to the eastern end of the islet and back along the lagoon beach would ensure a sound sleep upon his return.

The path was a lonely one; there was not a house of any sort along the outer beach, from one end of the islet to the other, but on so small a place there were trails everywhere, and this one was used by the men when fishing along the reefs, and often by the women when going to wash clothes after a rainfall, in the pools of fresh water among the rocks. The moon was well down toward the horizon, and de Laage was conscious of a feeling of solemn pleasure as he watched the silvery light flashing along the concave mirrors of the combers as they rose to crash down on the reef. There was a certain beauty in a low-island land and seascape on such a night: that he admitted; but there had been opportunity in his eighteen years of atoll service to enjoy it well past the point of weariness. How many times had he taken this same walk on just such nights? Not often, in late years; that was true. In fact, considering the matter, he could not remember having left the grounds of the Residency, after dinner, during the past year and more.

In half an hour he had almost reached the end of the islet. Crossing over the lagoon side, he

seated himself on the beach to watch the setting
moon, and remained there for some time, enjoying
a vacancy of mind refreshing and soothing after
his troubled reflections of the hour before. Turning his head presently for an idle glance across the
islet, he observed that someone was approaching
from the direction of the village. It was a lad who
moved at the quick, shuffling trot of the heavily
burdened, and who carried a pole over his shoulder with a five-gallon kerosene tin hanging at either end. The Administrator straightened his back
and turned to regard the intruder with an intent
stare. The policeman in him was suddenly very
wide-awake. What could this young fellow be doing at such an hour? What was he carrying in
those tins? Water, of course; they were used for
nothing else, but who could want water carried
here?

The lad passed in the moonlight without perceiving the watcher, and disappeared in the shadows of a thicket farther along the beach. De Laage
arose and followed him.

He came upon him as he was setting down his
burden alongside a large sailing canoe, concealed
among the trees at the water's edge. Suddenly
aware that he was not alone, the boy gave a vio-
lent start and seemed half-minded to make a run
for it. His expression of terror further aroused the
Administrator's suspicions. He glanced at his face,
revealed in the moonlight, and recognized him at
once. It was Mako, the young son of Tavi, who had
for some time been acting as the sailor and deck
hand on Father Paul's cutter.

"What are you doing here?" the Administrator
asked. The boy made no reply. De Laage bent
forward to look into the canoe. It had been packed
with supplies of various kinds: axes, fishing

spears, cooking utensils, bedding, with boxes and bundles carefully stowed away in all the available space. De Laage struck a match to examine the contents of the canoe more carefully. It contained a surprising assortment of things. He turned brusquely to the boy and repeated: "What are you doing here?"

Still there was no reply.

"Can't you speak? Tell me where you are going."

Mako hesitated and finally said, without raising his eyes: "To Motu Atea, monsieur."

The Administrator stared down at him. The copra cutting on Motu Atea had been finished well before the *Katopua's* arrival and the people had returned home. Why should this boy be preparing to go there at such an hour and with such a cargo?

"To Motu Atea? For what purpose? . . . Why are you going there?"

Mako made no reply, but continued to stand with his head down, staring at the ground between his feet. Impatient at his stubborn and nervous silence, de Laage ordered harshly: "Come with me."

He went along the path at a rapid walk, the boy following. It never so much as occurred to de Laage that he might run away, nor, in his terror and anguish of mind, did the thought occur to Mako. His awe of the Administrator was far too great to permit the slightest disobedience of his orders.

De Laage's mind was busy as he walked. A strange business, this. What the devil could the boy be up to? The chief himself had told him that the last of the copra makers had returned from

Motu Atea the week before. Why then should this boy be going there? He was lying, evidently; but for what purpose? What reason would he have. . . . All at once a stupefying thought crossed his mind. Terangi! By heavens, could it be possible? Was the fellow on Manukura, concealed on one of the islets? Why not? His wife was here, all his people were here. Who else would be so glad to shield him? There had been ample time, after these many weeks, for him to reach home. His complete disappearance from Tahiti could only mean that he had gotten clean away. De Laage felt a shiver passing down his spine. Good God! If this were true, they might make him the laughingstock of the colony: an administrator ignorant of the fact that a notorious criminal was hidden at the very seat of government, on an island whose land area was scarcely greater than a large farm!

The village was profoundly silent as they passed its scattered houses. Here and there a dim light showed through the chinks in the thatch, from a kerosene lamp turned low, left burning as a protection against evil spirits, but the inmates were sleeping. Not so, however, in the house of Mama Rua. Marama was crouched near the door, left slightly ajar, watching for Mako's return. Hearing footsteps crunching over the coral gravel, she opened the door an inch or two wider. The forms of the two passers-by were indistinct in the starlight, but as they passed the house she had them in clear relief for an instant against the surface of the lagoon. With her keen sight she recognized them at once. She gave a little gasp of horror as she closed the door softly.

"Mama!" she exclaimed in a whisper. "Aué, Mama!"

The old woman crept forward in the darkness to her daughter-in-law's side. "What is it? Who passed? There were two."

"Monsieur de Laage! He has Mako with him!"

"*Éaha?*"

"It was Monsieur de Laage! I couldn't mistake him!" She sprang to her feet. "I must tell Father!"

Mama Rua gave an exclamation of anguish, pressing her hands tightly together. "Wait, child! He may know nothing. Follow them! Keep well hidden! Hide by a window and listen. Make haste! I will tell your father."

Next moment Marama was gone, running lightly in the shadows alongside the road.

Followed by the terrified Mako, de Laage reached his house, stepped softly on to the verandah, entered his office, and lit the lamp. He placed a chair for the boy so that the light would shine full in his face and motioned him to sit there. He seated himself in his swivel chair, with his back to the lamp. The lad gave him a brief terror-stricken glance and then sat with his hands tightly clasped, gazing at the floor.

"Your name is Mako, eh?" the Administator began, in the dry, inquisitorial manner he knew so well how to assume. "Now, Mako, I want the truth. Where were you going with that canoe?"

The lad made no answer.

"You shall not leave this room until you have told me, understand that," de Laage went on, "and it will be the worse for you if you keep me waiting long. Answer me! For whom were those things in the canoe? Who told you to put them there?"

An agonized silence was the only reply. As the Administrator sprang to his feet, feigning more anger than he felt, the door opened and Madame de Laage appeared, in her kimono.

"What is it, Eugene?" she asked.

He explained briefly, and then said: "Since I have had the misfortune to waken you, perhaps you will stop for a minute and help me. It may be that this boy understands less French than I supposed. Be good enough to ask him in his own language where he was going. Tell him there is no good in his lying. I will have the truth!"

Madame de Laage turned to Mako, smiled encouragingly, and questioned him in a gentle voice. He tried to meet her eyes, but could not, and answered briefly, in a whisper almost inaudible.

"He says he was going to Motu Atea."

"Nonsense! So he told me. I'll have no more of this! He understands French as well as yourself. Tiens! I'll soon have the truth!"

Swinging about in his chair once more, he faced the boy sternly.

"Look me in the face, Mako! Look up, I say!" Slowly the lad raised his head. "For whom were those things in the canoe?"

Mako opened his mouth, but no words came. He tried to lower his gaze, but the Administrator's eyes held his in a kind of hypnotic spell. The expression on his face, revealed in the full light of the lamp, was pitiful.

"Shall I answer for you?" de Laage asked, sternly. "Shall I tell you for whom they were designed?" He paused, subjecting the lad's face to a merciless scrutiny. "For Terangi! He is here! You know it!"

The expression on Mako's face was enough. If the boy had written and signed a statement of all he knew, of all he had hoped to accomplish, the confession could scarcely have been more complete.

Marama, who had been crouching outside the open window, sank down with her head in her arms at the mention of Terangi's name. In an instant she had overcome her agitation. She stole down the verandah steps, passed through the gate like a shadow, and ran toward her father's house at a pace few of the young men of the village could have equaled.

The Administrator glanced at his wife. His face was impassive; what went on in his mind was another matter.

"When did he come?" he then asked. "Answer me, boy! How did he get here?"

Mako was at the end of his self-possession. He mumbled in a voice, terrified and indistinct: "On the cutter."

"The cutter? Whose cutter? Germaine, what cutters have come in since I have been away?"

"Only Father Paul's."

De Laage gave a gasp of dismay. He turned sharply to Mako taking the boy's chin in his hand, raising his head until he could look him full in the face. "Mako, do you mean to tell me that Terangi came here with you, on Father Paul's cutter?"

The lad made no reply.

Chapter
7

Mako sat huddled in his chair, a look of unutterable misery and desolation upon his face. Madame de Laage herself was profoundly distressed. You can imagine her astonishment upon learning what the boy had been forced to betray. As she glanced at her husband, she was conscious of a feeling almost of hatred for him, and of loathing for herself as his instrument. With her warm heart and quick intelligence, she was able to visualize the misery that would be brought into the lives of Terangi's family—the grief that everyone on the island would feel at his recapture. And yet, what else could the Administrator have done? He could hardly be expected to close his eyes and allow an escaped prisoner to go his ways.

De Laage halted and turned to Mako.

"You will remain in this room," he said, "until you have my permission to leave it."

The lad made no reply. "You understand, Mako?" Madame de Laage asked, gently, addressing him in the native tongue. There was a look of piteous appeal in his eyes as he glanced up at her. He gave a barely perceptible nod and again stared at the floor.

"Madame de Laage will stay here with you," the

{ 87 }

Administrator added. "Understand! You will be severely punished if you disobey me!"

Mako's heart was so numbed with despair at what he had been forced to disclose that the warning was quite needless. There could be no saving Terangi now: that he knew. The harm was done.

De Laage called his wife outside the room for a moment, shutting the door behind them.

"I'm sorry, my dear," he said. "There is no help for it. I must ask you to remain with him. If the boy should bolt, let me know at once. You can send Arai. But no . . . that won't do. You will have to come yourself. I shall be at Father Paul's."

"You need have no fears," Madame de Laage replied. "I know Mako. He will do as I say."

The Administrator was a man of unalterable habit, scrupulously exact in performing all the little routine duties of life. He rose, customarily, at precisely six o'clock, arrayed himself in an old-fashioned bathing costume of blue flannel, put on his dressing gown and slippers, and stepped out to the lagoon beach. There he would swim clumsily for fifteen minutes, a few yards offshore, and then return to his bathroom, a small detached building containing a fresh-water shower, connected with the dwelling house by a covered passageway. Fresh water is precious on all the low islands and limited to what rain water is caught from those houses provided with tin roofs. On Manukura there were three cement reservoirs: a large communal one which received the water from the roof of the church, another at the chief's house, and a third, a one-thousand-gallon tank, at the Residency, supposed to be for the use of the Administrator's family alone. But he was as unselfish as he was just and precise in the performance of his duties, and in times of scarcity the water in his reservoir was for the use of all the village, in carefully rationed quantities, according to the size of the household needing it. His own received no more than the others. Even in times of plenty, when the tank was full to overflowing, he limited himself to two gallons for his morning shower, drawing off in a pitcher this amount, which he placed in the container overhead. But first he would shave, using a pint of water for this purpose. He had a razor case, lined with black velvet, in which were seven razors, one for each day of the week. He had, I am sure, a secret contempt for any man who used a safety razor, and took pride in the fact that he shaved without a mirror. His hand was as steady as a rock, and I must do him the credit to say that no barber could have made a better job of it. This task finished, he would have his shower and dress for the new day in white ducks, well starched and crackling. One of the trials of Madame de Laage's life, upon their first coming to Manukura, had been to find a native woman who could launder her husband's clothes to his satisfaction, and a maid who would lay out a fresh suit in the evening, precisely where and in the manner in which he wished to find it.

These matters are by the way. I speak of them to give you a side view of his character. Little things were as important to him as large ones. Don't mistake me; I am not poking fun at him. I had great respect for him, and I will venture to say that, during the war, France had no more dependable and fearless battalion commander throughout her armies. He brought the same trustworthy, unimaginative qualities with him as Administrator of the Tuamotu. Had it not been so, he would, certainly, on this particular morning, have proceeded at once with his investigation, without making his usual careful toilet for the coming day.

He may, in fact, have omitted the sea bath, but that was the only omission. Having left Madame de Laage, he shaved, had his two-gallon shower, and dressed carefully and methodically in the fresh suit Arai had laid out for him the previous evening. It was still dark. He put on his sun helmet and was about to take his electric flash lamp, but thought better of this. The village was asleep, and he wished no one to be aroused and curious as to his movements until he had seen Father Paul. It did not occur to him, apparently, that there could be any immediate danger of Terangi's escape.

He was unspeakably shocked at what he had learned from Mako. That the priest should have brought Terangi, a fugitive from justice, to Manukura without immediately reporting the man's presence was a breach of faith inconceivable to the Administrator. In fact, he could scarcely believe it possible. Might not Mako, in his confusion, have assented to something that had no basis in truth? He had put the direct question to him. In his terror, the boy might have replied without knowing what it was he had affirmed, and, growing more confused, have been unable to correct the mistake. The Administrator recalled that, some years before, three Manukura boys had been caught making off with a small cutter belonging to one of their fathers. Their purpose had been to sail to Tahiti, to see the sights of the great capital. They had heard of motor cars, of motion pictures, of many marvelous things unknown on Manukura. They had wanted to see them for themselves, and were not in the least daunted by the thought of a

600-mile voyage. Mako had had a wide experience in sailing from island to island with Father Paul. He was a bold lad and might easily be the ringleader in another madcap boyish venture. The large canoe was provisioned as though for just such a voyage.

De Laage halted. It might be that. It might well be that. He was uncertain whether to go on or to turn back for a further questioning of Mako. Then he recalled the boy's manner, the anguish and terror in his face. No, it must be that Terangi was here. And had not Father Paul avoided him ever since his return? For the first time in years he had not come to dinner at the Residency.

The Administrator proceeded toward the church, crossing the depression in the land that almost divided the islet on the footbridge made of two squared coconut logs laid side by side. For all his disturbed mind, he had time for a moment of annoyance that Fakahau had not yet replaced the broken handrail. Before his departure from Manukura, months before, he had asked that this be done. He made a mental note of the matter. That handrail was to be made usable before another day had passed.

Upon reaching Father Paul's little house, he hesitated for a moment, and then knocked firmly. The priest, like most elderly men, slept lightly, and was aroused at once. He got into his threadbare old *soutane,* put on his straw slippers, lighted his lamp, and came to the door, searching his mind as he did so as to which member of his flock might have need of his services at such an hour. He gave no outward indication of surprise upon finding the Administrator standing on the doorstep. As he entered, de Laage apologized for the untimely visit. His manner was administratorial—polite, but coldly formal and punctilious; it was not his customary manner in speaking with Father Paul. The priest brought forward his only easy chair and then seated himself on a wooden stool by his writing table. The little reception room was austere in its simplicity. The walls were whitewashed and bare save for a crucifix and a framed lithograph of Leo XIII which hung over the table. The only furniture consisted of the easy chair, the wooden stool, a bench for visitors, and the table holding an unshaded kerosene lamp.

A few perfunctory remarks passed, followed by a moment of awkward silence. De Laage cleared his throat.

"I must explain to you the purpose of this call," he began. "Late this evening, being unable to sleep, I walked to the far end of the *motu*. While there I chanced to see the boy, Mako, pass with two large tins of water on a carrying pole. I was curious as to what he could be doing at that hour and followed him. I found him placing the tins in the large sailing canoe belonging to the chief. The canoe was loaded with supplies and provisions of all sorts. The boy was greatly confused at my questions and made replies which I knew were false. I took him with me to the Residency and questioned him further. The confession he as good as made to me is incredible."

He paused. Father Paul sat with one sturdy brown hand resting lightly on the table, his childlike blue eyes regarding de Laage steadily. The Administrator's gaze was fixed upon the portrait of Pope Leo.

"And the confession was . . . ?" the priest asked.

"That the escaped prisoner, Terangi, had been brought to this island in your cutter."

"It is true," the priest remarked, quietly.

"You are telling me that the prisoner is now at liberty, on Manukura? May I ask why I have not been informed?"

"Monsieur l'Administrateur, a priest of the Church has duties to perform that differ from your own. Such a duty is concerned here."

De Laage's pale face flushed and he stared at the priest incredulously.

"He may, then, consider it his duty to harbor a fugitive, a murderer, no less; to set at defiance the just laws of the State and those who are sworn to enforce them?"

"He may, under certain circumstances."

"And what are those circumstances?"

There was a note of appeal in the father's voice as he replied. "Monsieur de Laage, I have known Terangi his life long. I have known his parents and their parents before them. In all its branches, there is no family throughout the Archipelago more worthy of respect. This son, Terangi, is a deeply wronged young man. How he left Tahiti I do not know. I picked him up at sea, in my cutter, thirty miles from Manukura. He was clinging to a capsized canoe; the outrigger was gone. He had been clinging there for two days and a night. He had made a voyage of nearly six hundred miles in that small canoe that he might see his mother, his wife, and his little daughter. Those are the circumstances. Would you have had me give him up?"

"This deeply wronged young man, as you call him, has only himself to blame for the severity of his punishment. I am your fellow countryman; your Administrator, as you are my priest. I am your parishioner no less than he. What of the wrong you do to me?"

"The wrong . . . ?"

"I am here to enforce the law; and yet you

would keep this fugitive in hiding, at the very seat of the administration. If he succeeds in escaping elsewhere, I shall be held responsible, and justly so. It will be a blot upon my record that I shall never be able to remove. It may, quite possibly, mean the end of my career."

"I had not thought of that, my friend," the priest replied gently, after a moment of silence. "I am much to blame, and I ask your forgiveness. And yet, even if I had remembered, I could have done no other than I have done. But there shall be no blot upon your record. If a wrong has been committed, the fault is mine, and I shall take it upon myself."

The Administrator rose abruptly. "Father Paul, I will ask you one question," he replied, coldly. "Where is Terangi Matokia?"

"I do not know."

"You know that he is on Manukura?"

"I know that he *was* here; that I brought him here. But where he is now I do not know."

The Administrator took up his helmet, and, with a slight formal bow to the priest, turned and left the room.

You will understand that neither Fakahau nor Tavi had been idle during this time. At the moment when the Administrator passed in the street, with Mako, the chief and his brother had been upon the point of setting out for the end of the *motu*. The chief was waiting in the darkness at his house, with Tita asleep in his arms, when Marama came back from the Residency. They set out at once for the end of the *motu* where the canoe was moored. They reached the place in a quarter of an hour and by that time Fakahau had told his daughter what she must do. Their farewells were of the briefest.

Marama clung to her father for a moment, then, took her place in the stern of the canoe. The sail was quickly raised and made fast. Tita, awake now, puzzled to know what was happening, took her place beside her mother. Noiselessly, Fakahau pushed the canoe out into deep water, the light breeze caught the sail, and the long slim craft glided rapidly away to the south'ard. The chief stood in waist-deep water, looking after it until it vanished in the darkness. Wading ashore, he struck into a dim path that led through the groves inland, at some distance from the lagoon beach.

Dark as it was under the palms, he kept to the path by instinct, walking swiftly. Far down the motu he could see a light burning at the Residency. As he approached the settlement, he saw a second light appear in Father Paul's house and immediately guessed the reason for it. Mata, his wife, was waiting for him, in a small thatched hut that stood behind the chief's European dwelling. He entered by the doorway in the north end and called softly. Mata crossed the room and took his arm. "They have gone?" she asked quickly.

"Yes. The wind is at east, and light. There will be no danger of capsizing. Marama can handle the canoe as well as a man. They will be on Motu Tonga in less than an hour."

"And what then?" The chief could detect the note of intense anxiety in his wife's voice. "The Administrator knows that Terangi is here! The pass will be watched. Even though it were not, day will break before they could reach it."

"There is only one thing that can be done, and that I have arranged. Terangi and Marama will sink the canoe off the beach at Motu Tonga, in such a place that none could find it. Their supplies they will bury in the sand. The Administrator will search every *motu* along the reef, that is sure. And he will find no trace of them—nothing."

"But what of themselves? . . . *Aué!* I know! *Te Rua!*"

"They will hide there," said Fakahau. "He may search Motu Tonga, all the *motu*, until he is weary. He will never find them. Later, we can decide what is best to be done."

Mata seized her husband's arm. "Nothing could be better! He will believe they have escaped; gone elsewhere."

"What else can he believe? We will wait and see what he will do then."

They broke off their whispered conference upon hearing a knocking at the front door of their main house. Fakahau knew that knock, and the precise frame of mind of the man who thus announced himself. Under ordinary circumstances, he would immediately have put on his white trousers and coat, but in this instance he wanted it to appear that he had not recognized the summoner. He whispered to Mata: "Call out."

"*Ko vai tera?*" she demanded, shrilly, as though asking which of her neighbors might be making so untimely a call. The only reply was a repetition of the double knock, even louder than before.

Fakahau waited no longer. He went as he was, barefoot and dressed only in his *pareu*. Mounting the steps to his back verandah, he went along the hallway that divided the main dwelling house and lighted the lamp that hung from the ceiling in his front parlor.

Fakahau's European house was the pride of Manukura. Although he and his family spent little time in it, much preferring the cool native dwelling in the back yard, he felt that it was his duty as chief, for the honor and dignity of his people, to have exotic possessions worthy of his estate. His *salon* was a spacious, high-ceilinged room filled with ornate furniture: chairs and sofas upholstered in red and green plush, and tables with the tortured legs common in France a generation and more ago. Cheval mirrors stood in the corners, and others, gilt-framed and quite as large, hung from the walls. There were, also, oil paintings representing rustic scenes in Europe: stags that had proudly halted to pose for the artist against snowy backgrounds, French youths and maidens of the sixties and seventies, boating upon lakes or sitting pensively in gardens. I believe that Captain Nagle had bought the lot of them for Fakahau at an auction sale in Tahiti. Opposite the *salon* was a sumptuous state bedroom that had never been occupied by anyone save the Bishop on his single visit to Manukura. The bed was eight feet long and six wide and held a kapok mattress at least three feet thick. Have you ever slept on—or, better, in—an untufted kapok mattress? Probably not. There is nothing hotter in this world, nor, probably, in the next. The hopeful guest is rather pleased by the feel of it at first, as it snuggles itself around his weary body; then he sinks deeper and deeper and the sweat begins to pour out. Within half an hour, granted that he has been able to endure it for so long, he finds himself lying in a deep puddle of his own perspiration, for Kapok is wonderfully water-tight; and once the "give" has been taken up, there is nothing harder to lie upon. It is like being set in a bed of gradually solidifying cement. I can imagine what a glorious night the Bishop must have had. I was here at the time of his visit, and I recall that, the following day, he went through his round of duties and sat through the elaborate feast prepared for him with a decidedly glassy look in his eyes.

Forgive the digression. I can't help smiling, inwardly, when I think of Fakahau's state bedroom. But when I think of him and Mata, and that I shall never see them again, the smile vanishes. Two more admirable persons never lived.

Fakahau, having lighted the lamp, lost no time in going to the door. He wished, by his manner, to express surprise upon seeing who his visitor was, but this was lost on de Laage, who strode into the hallway and then halted, as in duty bound, until the chief should show him into the *salon*.

During the brief walk to the chief's house, there had been time to put a stern check upon his emotions. He was appalled, no less, at what he considered Father Paul's disloyalty, so deeply disturbed and angry that he felt it necessary to close the interview at once. He might have said something regrettable, beneath the dignity of an administrator to give voice to; and however unworthy the priest, his position must be respected. There was now no doubt in de Laage's mind that all Manukura, save only himself and his wife, had known of Terangi's return. He believed that Captain Nagle himself must have known as he sat at his table at dinner, the evening before. If Father Paul could shield this escaped criminal it could hardly be expected that Nagle would have a more scrupulous standard of honor. As for Fakahau, the man's father-in-law, it would be futile to ask him where Terangi was hidden. It was to be assumed that he knew. The line of action to be taken was clear-cut. By the time he had reached the chief's door, he knew what this should be.

Fakahau was a giant in stature, six feet four and a half, with strength in proportion to his size. De

Laage was a tall man, but he looked like a stripling beside the chief. Secretly he resented this contrast so unfavourable to the representative of France. He would have much preferred a smaller man for chief, one with less native dignity; but he had been compelled to resign himself to the fact that Manukura would have no other.

"Be seated, please," he said.

Fakahau did so, apologizing at the same time for his waistcloth. He spoke excellent French, having been reared in the household of a former administrator who, upon discovering his intelligence, took great pains to teach him. Polynesians have a language of courtesy equal to our own, and the chief was able to translate the forms of it with an ease that had always surprised de Laage. At this moment, it seemed the very language of subtle dissimulation. His heart was filled with anger, and it shocked him that a man should be able to hide so well his true thoughts and feelings. He listened coldly as Fakahau bridged the awkwardness of the moment. The first light of dawn was beginning to filter through the groves outside, although it was not yet strong enough to dim the light of the lamp. De Laage drew out his watch, consulted it, and held it in his hand as he spoke.

"I wish you to assemble all the people, excepting the small children, by the *himiné* house within half an hour's time," he said. "Every man and woman, the young people as well. No one is to be excused. You will also have all the canoes collected and drawn up on the beach near by. Dress and attend to this matter immediately. When you have done so, I will inform you and the others of my reason for wishing it."

He then rose and, with a slight cold nod to the chief, walked out of the room.

Chapter

8

The village was waking as de Laage left the chief's house. He walked to the beach and looked out over the lagoon. It lay empty to the gaze as far as he could see, placid and shimmering in the pale light of early morning. If Terangi was hidden on the village islet, de Laage was determined that he should not leave it unseen. He tore a leaf from his pocketbook and wrote a note to his wife, telling her of what he had arranged and asking her to send his binoculars. He sent the note by a lad who had just appeared from a nearby house, and walked slowly up and down the beach until the boy returned.

Meanwhile, Fakahau had promptly carried out the Administrator's orders. Messengers had been sent in both directions, and within a quarter of an hour all the settlement was astir. Until this morning, you will understand, Terangi's presence on the island was known to none of the natives outside his own family. By the time the people had assembled at the *himiné* house, everyone knew it —that is, all of the adults. There was no longer the possibility of secrecy, nor the need for it. Realizing this, Fakahau had seen to it that the news should be spread, not only that Terangi had come home, but that he was hidden, with his wife and daughter, in the cave they all knew on Motu Tonga. The Polynesian method of disseminating news is as swift as it can be secretive when there is need for secrecy. For all my years in the Archipelago, I do not yet know just how they manage this sort of thing. Little is said, but by slight gestures, glances, the intonation of the voice as they make elliptical comments to one another, everything is told. The chief well knew the loyalty of his people. There was no danger that any of them would search with the intent of discovering Terangi's hiding place.

All of the canoes were being assembled; young men and boys were paddling them in from both sides to the beach near the *himiné* house where they were drawn up in a long line, around fifty in all, taking large and small together. There were a dozen large sailing canoes, and two reef boats, each capable of holding a dozen men, which were used for the transport of copra from the various islets. De Laage paced the beach, watching over this carrying out of his orders, but speaking to no one. The chief, now dressed in an immaculate suit of white duck, wearing the sash of his office and with a broad-brimmed pandanus hat on his head, was among the men, superintending the alignment of the canoes which were drawn up for inspection. In the background, among the groves, the women and children and older people were gathered. You can imagine the astonishment felt by all at the news that had passed so swiftly amongst them, but had you seen their faces you would not have guessed at the emotion they so quietly concealed. In so far as any outward indication was concerned, they might have assembled there before going to church for one of their customary services. Only the children were in a state of excitement. They realized that something was up, but didn't, of course, know what it was.

Father Paul was present, but the Administrator gave no sign of having noticed him. I should like to have known what his thoughts were at that moment. Close as my contact with him was, I was never able to get upon terms even approaching intimacy with him. I suppose that he felt as warmly toward Father Paul as he could feel toward any man, yet I doubt whether the father knew him much better than I. He was not a man of delicate perceptions, but I sometimes felt, as I did on this occasion, that he was conscious of a vague irritation at his lack of rapport with the people he governed. He didn't in the least understand them. He may have admitted this to himself, sometimes, in the innermost secrecy of thought.

When all the canoes had been brought in, Fakahau reported to de Laage, who walked down the line, counting them and carefully scrutinizing each one. The large sailing canoe belonging to the chief was missing, of course. He remarked it, but said nothing.

The *himiné* house is a place of public meeting in Polynesia. On Manukura it was a pretty structure rounded at the ends and open at the sides; the roof of pandanus-leaf thatch was supported on pillars of *tohonu* wood. It was fifty feet long by twenty-five broad and the floor of coral sand was covered with mats. All the grown-ups now assembled there, and de Laage mounted the small platform, the chief beside him to act as interpreter. I was present that morning, not merely as an onlooker but as an unwilling participant in what followed. I was completely in the dark as to the purpose of this early gathering. Naturally, the natives had not informed me of the news the chief had passed on to them, and although de Laage had greeted me upon my arrival, he had not explained why he wanted me there. He merely asked me to sit with him and the chief on the platform. Captain Nagle alone was not present. De Laage was not devoid of tact, and he well knew how Nagle felt toward Terangi, who stood almost in the relationship of a son to him. The captain may have known, by this time, what was afoot, but throughout the whole of this day he remained aboard his schooner.

I was glad to accept de Laage's invitation, for a panorama of Manukura faces always interested me. I liked to let my glance wander from one to another, comparing them and the gathering as a whole with similar assemblies I had seen on other islands of the Group. There are, often, striking contrasts between the people of one island and those of another, so marked, even in these days, that one is led to believe that they are of different racial stock. That is the opinion of many ethnologists with respect to Polynesians in general. They recognize among the different groups at least four divergent racial types. There is no reason why this should not be so. These islands were peopled by successive waves of migrants from the West. When one remembers their ancient home, which was, almost certainly, India, and the many archipelagos that must have been halting places on their eastward migrations, the mixture of bloods is easily accounted for.

Whenever de Laage addressed the village as a whole, he spoke to them directly, as though assuming that they understood French. Fakahau would stand at his side, a little behind him. When a perceptible halt was made, the chief would know that he was expected to translate what had just been said. De Laage's face was stern and his manner impressive. He spoke briefly, informing the gathering that the escaped prisoner, Terangi, was somewhere hidden on Manukura. He did not accuse the people of knowing it, or assume by his manner that they must know of it. He spoke of Terangi's stubborn intractability as a prisoner, of his many escapes, made possible, he said, by the leniency toward him of the authorities on Tahiti. He had grossly abused their kindness. His original sentence was six months. Had he quietly submitted to it, he would have been free long since. By his willful foolishness he had increased this sentence by many years. At his last escape he had killed a prison guard. This fugitive the government was determined to recapture; if necessary they would dispatch the gunboat, stationed at Papeete, to apprehend him. Whatever the attitude of Manukura might be toward him, it was the solemn duty of every man and woman to assist their Administrator in his recapture. A search of the atoll was now to be made, and he expected them to fulfill that duty.

The people listened in deepest silence, and when de Laage had finished, not a question was asked, not a comment made. I observed Tavi, who sat directly below the platform, his hands clasped over his huge solid belly; he was listening with the placid attention he might have given to one of Father Paul's sermons. The others were as quietly attentive. De Laage then dismissed them, to await his orders outside. It was then that he asked my assistance in making the search. He himself would lead the party to search the village islet. If Terangi were not found here, he would proceed along the northern reefs to Motu Atea. He asked me to take charge of a second party to go along the opposite side of the atoll, by way of Motu Tonga. He regretted having to commandeer my services, but there was no one else he could trust, and two search parties were essential if Terangi was to be caught.

Never have I had such an unpleasant task. It was outside my province as a medical officer, and my sympathies were all with Terangi. But I could not refuse, although, technically, I would have been justified in doing so. The Administrator was in a difficult situation. The search had to be made, and no native could be put in charge of either party. The chief was to remain behind, in the settlement.

There were twenty-five in my party, men and youths together. We set out for Motu Tonga in the two reef boats. Each rowed six oars, but there was a good breeze and we proceeded under sail. Tavi was with me and his son-in-law, Farani, a lad of twenty. After five years on Manukura I knew everyone, of course. I was *"Taoté"*—Doctor—to all of them, and they had come to accept me without reserve. It went sorely against the grain with me to be sent on such an expedition as this. I well knew how they loathed it. Nevertheless, I was bound that our work should be done thoroughly.

There was a charming cove at the western end of Motu Tonga, on the lagoon side. It was the customary landing place. We reached it in an hour and a half. I smile as I look back to that morning and see myself there with my men gathered around me. Ceremonial plays a great part in native life, and a little speech-making is the preliminary to all communal activity. I was rather pleased with myself at the fortright, straight-from-the-shoulder manner in which I addressed my men. I told them that Terangi was certain to be caught. There was no escaping the long arm of the law. Whatever we, as individuals, might think of the injustice of his imprisonment, we should only harm him by the attempt to shield him. Ours was an unpleasant task, but, as the Administrator had said, if we failed to perform it, the Governor of Tahiti would order the man-of-war stationed there to come to Manukura. Failure in our duty would only postpone a little the evil day for Terangi, and so forth, and so forth. I must have talked for a good five minutes. The Administrator himself would have highly approved of this Voice of Duty speaking through the mouthpiece of his medical officer.

Then we got on with the duty itself. I extended my men in a single line, stretching across the motu from ocean to lagoon beach. I took my position toward the centre and behind it, so that I could make sallies to one side and the other, keeping my eye upon them all; and I had my binoculars so that I could bring the more distant men directly before me. I was surprised at the thoroughness with which they went about the business; more particularly, at Tavi's hearty coöperation. They really did search, and carefully. They beat every small thicket; examined each of the old tou and pukatea and purau trees. These, with the scattered coconut palms, were the most likely hiding places, and I saw to it that they were well explored as we proceeded. Between, were clumps of scrub, none of which were missed, but the islet, for the most part, was free from thick undergrowth and you had clear views across the four-hundred-yard extent from the inner to the outer beach. I flattered myself that I was an efficient, painstaking leader of a search party. Although I kept close watch, I saw no footprints in the sand, except those I judged to be our own. I could not, of course, be everywhere at once, but by the time we had reached the eastern end of Motu Tonga, I was convinced that Terangi was not there.

I had left four boys to sail the reef boats to that end of the islet. They were awaiting us, and we immediately set out, just inside the reef, in the direction of Motu Atea. "Atea"—it is a name I love, meaning "distant," "far-off," and well suited to the islet that enclosed the extreme eastern end of Manukura lagoon. It lies, as I may have said, twenty miles from the village islet, and is not visible from Motu Tonga. Between the two islets is mile after mile of bare reef where the long rollers of the Pacific batter themselves into foam and wind-driven spray. There are many unforgettable sights to be seen in a world so rich and varied as ours, but I know of none more memorable, and more awe-inspiring, than the view, from a small boat or canoe, of the surf piling over the reefs of a coral island. The best vantage point is from within the lagoon, close to the reef. There is no long feathering of the seas as they approach. On all low islands, the slope of the outer reef is scarcely a slope at all; it descends with astonishing steepness into the depths. The soundings only a short distance offshore are in hundreds of fathoms, and a mile beyond, the lead must descend a thousand before fetching bottom. For this reason the combers are almost upon you before they break, and the thread of the reef, often no more than fifteen or twenty yards across, seems no protection at all.

On the morning of our search, there was a surprisingly heavy surf along the reef. I call it surprising, for there had been no wind to account for it. The men in my boat were as glad as myself to have some topic of conversation other than Terangi; we discussed the surf, trying to account for the huge swell that had set in.

"It's not from the south'ard," Maunga said. "You can see that for yourself, Doctor."

Old Kauka, who was sitting beside me at the tiller, nodded.

"É. It'll be heavier than this along the northern reefs. That's where it's coming from: northeast. There's been dirty weather off there."

Tavi fancied himself as a weather prophet, and I must do him the justice to say that his predictions were usually accurate.

"Has been?" he replied. "My belief is that we have it to come. Shouldn't wonder if we were held up two or three days on Motu Atea before we can get back to the settlement. See how the wind's veering round. It's due west, now. If it keeps on like this it'll kick up a heavy sea inside the lagoon."

Tavi was right, although I had not before noticed the change in the wind. It was blowing straight from the west, and we were running before it briskly. Far ahead of us, inconceivably lonely against the vast background of the sea, was a tiny *motu* which the natives called Frigate Bird Islet. At the rate we were going it didn't take us long to come abreast. It was about three hundred yards long by one hundred across. Two ancient coconut palms, a few scattered *miki-miki* and pandanus trees, and some clumps of low green bush made up the vegetation of the islet. I loved this place. When I first came to Manukura, and it seemed that I could never have enough of solitude, I used to go there, alone, and stay for three or four days at a time. It lies sixteen miles from the village, diagonally across the lagoon. I would cross in a small sailing canoe with food and water on board, and a small tent to shelter me from the midday sun. The heat was terrific from eleven until four, but I put up with that for the sake of the early mornings and evenings—above all, the nights.

I don't know whether you're a lover of poetry? I am; always have been. During the war it was my unfailing consolation in a world gone mad save for the poets. You may think it strange, but I love English poetry better than our own. Ours has a subtlety, a perfection in the expression of complicated shades of thought, which their poets are sometimes foolish enough to try to imitate. Why should they try when they have their own inimitable virtues? Beauty—the thing itself, gushed out of the hearts of their best poets as limpid as spring water, and what is poetry without it? The other virtues count for nothing. But what I was about to say is that during the darkest period of the war— the early spring of 1918—a young English lieutenant, badly wounded,—I had sawed off both legs for him—gave me a book of verse, recently published, by a man named Hodgson, Ralph Hodgson. I was first struck by that; couldn't imagine a fellow with such a name being anything but a grocer or a bus driver. But it has no significance in this case. There was one poem that particularly appealed to me. It was called "The Song of Honor," and it ended with these lines:—

> I stood and stared; the sky was lit,
> The sky was stars all over it,
> I stood, I knew not why,
>
> Without a wish, without a will,
> I stood upon that silent hill
> And stared into the sky until
> My eyes were blind with stars, and still
> I stared into the sky.

So it was with me on my lonely nights on Frigate Bird Islet, except that there was no hill to stand on. I lay on my back on that tiny island, with all the Pacific around me and the whole vault of the heavens arching over me, and stared myself half-blind with stars. I shouldn't wonder if I've been a bit queer ever since my first experience there. No doubt you have felt the impact in a different way during your African service. It's not unpleasant—at least, I don't find it so. But it is—what shall I say? —chastening.

I'm forgetting Terangi. We didn't find him on Frigate Bird Islet. From any signs that appeared, man might never have set foot there since the day of creation. What we did find were the tracks of a huge turtle which had laid her eggs there not earlier than the night before. What a loss was that! If there is anything Low Islanders love it is turtle steak. At times when they were caught, on Manukura, all the village made holiday, and nothing more was done until the successive turtle feasts were over. These feasts are survivals from heathen times when turtle was the only meat, except sea fowl, which Tuamotu folk had. My men forgot Terangi in the keenness of their disappointment at arriving too late to capture this one. However, they filled a five-gallon tin with the eggs, which we carried with us.

We had another small islet to search and then nothing but five more miles of surf-battered reef until we reached Motu Atea. With a fresh following wind we made excellent time and landed at the southern end of the large islet at half-past three in the afternoon. The Administrator had instructed mè to begin the search at this end. If his party did not find Terangi on the village islet, they were to proceed directly to Motu Atea and work from the

northern end toward my own. There were no
lands along the entire stretch of the northern reef
between the settlement and Motu Atea.

We proceeded slowly, and the men showed the
same surprising willingness to search. I began to
think that either the Administrator's speech or my
own, or both together, had taken effect, and that
the men realized the futility of any attempt on
Terangi's part to escape. Presently we came to a
coral-cement storehouse used for tools and supplies of various kinds for the needs of the community when making copra on this islet. On the
rafters were laid fish spears, spare outrigger
booms and masts for the sailing canoes, and there
were cases of beef, balls of sinnet cord, spools of
line, blocks, sail twine, tar, paint, and the like.
Manukura folk had abundant supplies of this sort.
Unlike many Polynesians, they took great care of
their possessions, particularly all the gear for their
canoes, which they kept in perfect order. Several
hundred spare copra bags were stacked in a corner. Having made certain that Terangi was not
concealed here, we proceeded northward and, two
hours later, met de Laage's party near the center
of the islet.

Terangi had not been found. De Laage walked
aside with me while the members of the two parties gathered on the beach, squatting on their
haunches, native fashion, to await further orders.
I was sweaty and bedraggled, but the Administrator was nearly as immaculate as he had been
early that morning. He never perspired, even on
the hottest days. I often wondered, in a manner
half-envious, half-professional, if there wasn't
something amiss with his pores.

He was greatly upset, in his calm way, over our
double failure, and questioned me closely as to the

method of procedure I had taken with my party. He had confidence in me, that I knew; but feared that my men might have found opportunities to skimp the search. I set his mind to rest on that point. He too had been surprised at the apparent willingness of the men to find Terangi if he was to be found.

"There is only one explanation," he said, with an air of finality. "They know that he has escaped —left the island."

"You are convinced that he was not missed on the village islet?" I asked.

"Wholly convinced," he replied. "Even the church was examined. This I could not have done, had not the priest himself suggested it."

Never before had I heard him refer to Father Paul except by name. His speaking of him as "the priest" showed me how deeply the father lay under his displeasure.

"Not only is Terangi gone, but he has taken his wife and child with him," he continued. "The large canoe belonging to the chief is missing. They have gone, the three of them. More than likely he was close by when I discovered the boy, Mako, putting supplies into the canoe. While I was questioning the boy at the Residency, he must have gathered up wife and child and sailed out of the pass in the darkness."

A stern reproach to himself, for not having foreseen and forestalled this possibility, was implied in his manner.

"We must return to the settlement immediately," he said. "There is only one thing to be done. I must commandeer the *Katopua* and proceed with the search, elsewhere."

"Where shall you go?" I asked.

"First, to Amanu. I can almost promise myself

that he will be found there. He would sail for the nearest island. With the threatening weather now making up, he would not dare go elsewhere. He may be compelled to remain at Amanu for several days before he can push on. In any case, I shall seize him at one of four islands: Amanu, Hao, Aki Aki, or Vahitahi."

I confess that I was no more eager than the men to return at once to the village. We had had a hard day and very little to eat, and the thought of paddling and rowing up the twenty-mile lagoon in the teeth of the wind was anything but a pleasant one. It had veered round a bit more, toward the southwest, but there was not enough of a slant to enable us to use our sails. But the Administrator put aside the suggestions of Tavi and Kauka that we should delay our departure a little. Nor would he come with my party in one of the reef boats, much more comfortable to travel in, in such a heavy sea as had now made up. He preferred to remain with his own party.

As we set out, the sun was just setting in a weird-looking sky, overcast with a dirty yellowish haze through which the last light of day shone wanly. We made headway slowly. The sailing canoes, with their high sides, are awkward to paddle, and we soon left them far behind. But when we were no more than half an hour from Motu Atea, the wind chopped around to full southwest. It was welcomed with joy by the weary men. We made sail, thinking how lucky we were, but immediately we had, the wind died away to the lightest of airs, not enough to give our heavily laden boats steerageway. Down came the sails and out went the oars once more. The men rowed in disgruntled silence, broken only by the solid thud of the waves against our bow, each one like a brusque, powerful hand, checking our little way as it passed. *"Hoé, lads! Hoé!"* said Tavi. "Put your backs into it. It won't be for long."

"Éahahoia!" one of the rowers exclaimed. I have always loved that mouth-filling native expression, which means so many different things, according to the inflection of the voice from the mouth that it filled. It expresses astonishment, dismay, incredulity, anger, vexation—almost any shade of emotion can be voiced with the one word. On this occasion it meant: "It's all very well for you to say '*Hoé*,' you fat storekeeper! Why don't you do a little rowing yourself? And what do you mean, it won't be for long? Only until tomorrow morning!"

But Tavi had not gained his reputation as a weather prophet without deserving it. Presently the wind sprang up again, from due east, this time, and it blew more and more freshly. Tavi said nothing, but it amused me to see the expression on his face. There was pride in it, and supreme contempt for the *Éahahoia* exploder as he turned to me and remarked: "It will come full circle, Doctor, before it's done, but we'll be at the village long before that. I don't like the look of the sky," he added as he took the sheet.

Now we tore along at a splendid clip. The other reef boat was just abreast of us and we made a race of it, the men shouting taunting comments as one or the other gained a little advantage. And then came the canoes that we had left so far behind, with their great wings spread, their wakes creamy white, and their sharp bows sending the spray high in the air. We were doing a good seven knots, but the four of them passed us, one after the other, as though we were standing still. In a stiff breeze, a Tuamotu canoe will sail at from twelve to fifteen knots. They made a splendid sight as they passed, men on the outrigger runways, ready to shift at a second's notice to the hull side or the outrigger side as the strong gusty wind heeled them down. Those at the steering paddles leaned against their huge blades, but all had time to yell derisively at us as they went seething by. Ten minutes later they were lost to view in the gathering dusk.

Chapter
9

The northwest wind grew stronger during the night, making up in squalls that drummed furiously on de Laage's tin roof. These were followed by sudden calms, while sheet lightning played along the horizon and the rising sea made itself heard along the reef. Dawn revealed low gray clouds scudding above a leaden sea, and palm tops whipping and thrashing to the gusts.

De Laage was up before his usual time. On the way to his bathroom he stopped for a glance at the gauge on his water tank which he found had been filled by the night's rains. Then he peered at the recording barometer in its case. The glass stood a little low, yet at a level more or less normal for this time of year. No doubt this was only another of the northeasters the natives call *faarua*, which would blow itself out in a day or two. The equinox was at hand; one always expected uncertain weather at that time. When he had shaved and dressed, he joined his wife in the dining room, where coffee was already on the table.

"You still mean to go, Eugene?" she asked anxiously.

"I must," he replied.

"But what of the weather? It looks threatening to me."

"Nothing but a northeaster. Has Arai taken my note to Captain Nagle?"

"Yes. He's coming."

A moment later they saw the captain turn in at the gate. Another heavy squall drove down from the north. The captain halted on the verandah to remove his oilskins and sou'wester hat. De Laage stepped to the door to meet him.

"Come in, Captain. I'm sorry to trouble you so early. Germaine, pour the Captain a cup of coffee."

"I can do with a second cup this morning. A wet night, eh? There'll be water and to spare in the tanks this morning."

"How does it look to you?"

"The weather? Nothing to worry about. My glass is at twenty-nine eighty."

The Administrator nodded with a chilly smile. "I'll come straight to the point, Captain. I've asked you to come here to tell you that I must commandeer your schooner in the name of the Government. I may need her for a week, or a fortnight."

"This a bit sudden," Nagle replied ruefully. "I'd expected to leave for Fakahina to-morrow."

"The need is sudden," de Laage replied. "You shall lose nothing by this, of course. When can you be ready to sail?"

"Where do you wish to go?"

"To Amanu, first, and I hope only there. You will guess my errand. I must find Terangi. If he is not at Amanu we shall have to visit the neighboring islands as well."

The captain was silent for a moment. "I'll take you, of course," he said. "A man can't argue with the Government. We've nothing more to unload. I can be ready when you like."

"Then I shall be aboard in half an hour's time, if that's not hurrying you too much?"

Madame de Laage accompanied her husband to the dock. They found Tavi awaiting them there, with a cage of laths in which squatted a full-grown frigate bird. It was a strange and beautiful creature, smoothly feathered in black, shaded with chocolate, with a long, hooked beak and round unwinking eyes of velvet brown in which glittered pupils black as ink. De Laage often took one of Tavi's tame frigate birds on his tours of the Group, in case he wished to send a letter home. Tavi carried the cage aboard while the Administrator turned to bid good-bye to his wife. "I shall soon be back, my dear," he said in his matter-of-fact voice. "Don't wait to see us out of the pass. There's another squall coming; you've just time to reach the house."

A quarter of an hour later, with her engine going and her foresail set, the *Katopua* was headed for the passage, heeling a little to the gusts.

In a hidden nook among the piled-up bags of copra in his father's shed, poor little Mako had passed a night of misery such as only adolescents know. He had not tasted food since the day before and had slept only in snatches broken by troubled dreams. He felt that he could never again show his face in the village, and longed heartily to die. Twice during the previous afternoon he had heard his mother calling him, but had made no response. He had heard the sounds of the schooner's departure, and peeping through a chink in the wall had seen her set sail. He knew that Terangi had not been caught. Now, seeing that the schooner was gone, with the Administrator on board, he felt a thrill of hope. All at once he re-

alized that he was starving, crawled out of his re-
treat, and stole cautiously to his mother's outdoor
kitchen, where he found a loaf of bread and a
leaf-wrapped package of baked fish. He was eating hastily when his mother appeared from the
store.

"*Eaha nei!*" she exclaimed. "Where have you
been? Come to the store. Fakahau is there in
search of you. We told him you were not here."

"What does he want of me?"

"He did not say."

"Let him continue to think that I am not here."

"*Atira!*" Marunga exclaimed, impatiently. "Is he
not the chief? Come!"

With sullen eyes and dragging feet, Mako followed his mother into the store. His face burned
with shame as the chief came forward and laid a
hand on his shoulder.

"The fault was not yours, Mako," he said. "That
we know. Think of it no more. You know where
they are to be found. You shall go and tell them
that Monsieur has gone. He will be absent for a
week, at least."

The boy swallowed hard and shook his head. "I
cannot."

"You can and you shall," his father put in. "Fakahau is right; it is fitting that you should be the
messenger." He turned to his brother. "But will
they be in the cave?"

"Yes," said Fakahau. "I told Marama that they
were not to stir out of it until I sent them word.
Now go, Mako. Off with you."

Much as he dreaded meeting Terangi, Mako
knew that he would have to go. He chose a light
canoe and cut a green coconut frond, making it
fast, upright, for a sail. Scarcely anyone was
aware of his departure, for the stormy weather

had driven most of the people indoors. Sitting at his steering paddle, while the strong northeast wind sent the canoe tearing through the chop, Mako half forgot his troubles in the exhilaration of speed. In less than an hour he had drawn his light craft up on the beach at Motu Tonga. Near the eastern end of the islet, an ancient storm had torn great blocks of coral from the reef and piled them, wedged together in disorder, over a part of the old reef in the lagoon. Beneath this species of roof, weighing hundreds of tons, and now decomposing on the surface and overgrown with coarse grass, lay the cave. Light and air filtered down through chinks between the boulders, and the only entrance was a hole a fathom deep in the lagoon. In heathen times, when Manukura was raided by war canoes from neighboring islands, the women and children had taken refuge in this place, which was called "Te Rua." Its existence was a secret never disclosed to outsiders. Not even Father Paul had been told of the cave.

Mako stripped off his shirt, tucked up his *pareu*, and pulled down the diving goggles held on his head by an elastic band. He drew in a series of long breaths as he waded out to where the coral dropped away vertically in a submarine cliff. Then, half expelling the air from his lungs, he plunged into the lagoon.

He perceived the entrance at once: a green cavern where a tall man might have stood upright without touching the coral overhead. Propelling himself with a diver's long, deliberate strokes, he entered the cavern and rose into Te Rua's black, still pool.

"*Ko vai tera?*" Mako shivered at the sound of Terangi's voice.

"It is I, Mako," he replied.

"Come, we are here." A match flared, disclosing Terangi's erect figure, and Marama and Tita seated on the ledge. Then the match winked out, leaving the boy blind until his eyes grew accustomed to the faint light in the cave. With a sinking heart, he swam to where Terangi stood and pulled himself up on the clean dry sand of the ledge.

"Well?" said Terangi.

"Fakahau sent me. Monsieur has gone with the schooner to Amanu. He will not return before a week is up. Terangi . . ."

Mako could say no more. He sat huddled with his hands around his knees. He could not see the kindly expression in Terangi's eyes as he looked at him.

"Mako, do you remember the cigarette you made for me four days ago, in the cutter? It was my first smoke in many weeks. And before I swam ashore you gave me your tin of tobacco with your papers and matches. I have it here. Your hands are wet. Shall I make a cigarette for you?"

The boy was unable to speak for the joy and relief he felt. Marama patted his shoulder. "We know, Mako," she said. "What could any boy have done confronted by such a man? There is no anger in Terangi's heart, nor in mine. Come, let us get out of here."

Six-year-old Tita was the first to go. She was like a fish in the water, but her mother was close beside her as she dived. Terangi and Mako followed, and a few moments later they were all on the beach. Terangi glanced at the windward horizon and shrugged his shoulders as he glanced at Marama. She proceeded to dig out their buried property from its hiding place in the sand, while

Mako helped Terangi to float the sunken canoe. It was filled with lumps of coral and lay in two fathoms of water. After they had dived repeatedly, each time removing a stone or two, the canoe rose to the surface and they pulled it ashore. Presently they had collected all their hidden possessions.

"You can go nowhere in such weather," Mako ventured to remark.

"We must be patient," Terangi replied. "The storm will blow itself out in two or three days."

"Where shall you go then?" the lad asked, wishing next moment that he had not spoken. Terangi gave Marama a warning glance.

"It will be best to hide on one of the islands to leeward until the trade wind sets in strong and true. Then, perhaps, we shall sail to Rakahanga or Manihiki, or some other British island far to the west."

"Aye, that will be best," Mako replied eagerly. "There, Terangi, they could never find you!"

"Come, you two," said Marama. "We must hasten to make a hut. Mako, cut the fronds. I will plait them while Terangi puts up the framework."

The weather grew steadily worse. The wind hauled slightly to the north, blowing with ever-increasing force, and by late afternoon a heavy swell began to roll in from the northeast. The squalls had ceased; the trees swayed and bent to the wind which hummed through the streaming palms with an ever-rising note, while a procession of dark ragged clouds scudded by close overhead. Alone at the Residency, Madame de Laage had made fast all the doors and windows save those on the south side. The thought of her husband at sea worried her, and she admitted to herself that she was equally worried because of Terangi and his family. They had, undoubtedly, gotten through the pass during the dark hours of the day before, and must have reached Amanu long since if they had gone that way; but Madame de Laage was by no means so sure as her husband that Amanu was their destination. Although she had said nothing to him about it, she thought it more likely that Terangi would leave both Amanu and Hao to leeward and make for more distant islands: Paraoa or Ahunui. Paraoa, as she knew, was an uninhabited island belonging to the people of Hao; it would afford an excellent temporary refuge, but if they had gone that way the canoe would still be at sea. She shuddered at the thought of a sailing canoe being abroad in such weather. They would be lost if they capsized; Terangi and Marama alone could never right so large a canoe.

For the tenth time that day she stepped out to the sheltered south verandah to peer at the glass. Though it was not yet five o'clock, it was already so dark that she was obliged to return for her flashlight. She carefully studied the little wavering line on the coordinate paper. Instead of the customary slight rise after four o'clock, the barometer had continued to drop, and now stood at 29:50, the lowest she had ever seen it on Manukura. She tapped the case slightly; the instrument responded by dropping to 29:45.

The barometer at the Residency was the only one on the island. I myself called to consult it at this time, and found Madame de Laage still bending over the glass. Although far from easy in mind, I did my best to reassure her, saying that while we were probably in for a gale, there was no reason for believing that anything worse was on the way.

There would be time to think of that if the glass should drop below twenty-nine. "You need have no fears for the *Katopua*," I added. "Long before this time, Nagle will have her safe at anchor inside Amanu lagoon."

Outwardly, Madame de Laage was calm enough, but I knew that she was anything but reassured. She insisted on making me some tea, and while we were drinking it, in the dining room, questioned me about hurricanes. I told her what I had learned from my books on meteorology.

How these tropical revolving storms originate is still largely a matter of conjecture, but the places of their origin are well known: the belts of doldrums on either side of the Line. Hurricanes revolve counter-clockwise in the Northern Hemisphere, clockwise in the Southern, and it is believed, with some reason, that this is due to the trade winds blowing in toward the Equator from northeast and southeast. In the region of the Tuamotu, these storms nearly always come out of the north. Some travel only a few miles in the course of a day; others move southward at a speed the fastest ship could not equal. I discussed these matters with Madame de Laage in a manner of scientific detachment, but I refrained from mentioning one thing that was beginning to disquiet me: the fact that a steadily increasing wind from one quarter, accompanied by a dropping glass, indicates, in the case of a hurricane, that the observer is squarely on its track.

At that time, however, I did not seriously believe that we were in danger. I had seen other storms, as bad as this, blow themselves out within thirty-six hours, with no greater damage than a few trees uprooted and a cookhouse or two blown down. There were acres of tall old coconut palms

around the village which must have been planted
fifty years before: proof that hurricanes were by
no means common here. To be sure, they had
swept other islands of the Group much more recently. I had often heard the natives speak of the
great storms of 1903 and 1906. That of 1906 had
all but destroyed Hikueru and its neighboring islands, and had done great damage to the Society
Group as well. But Manukura seemed to be out of
the zone of most of these storms. I reminded Madame de Laage of the island's long immunity, and
despite the low barometer, she herself was not, I
think, seriously worried. At the moment, she was
much more concerned about Mama Rua than
about the weather. The day before, when we were
searching the island for Terangi, his mother had
taken to her bed, and when I saw her, not twelve
hours later, I had no doubt that she was dying. I
made shift to take her pulse and found it alarm-
ingly weak. I should have been glad to give her a
stimulant, but refrained even from suggesting this.
The people were willing to call upon me at most
times, but I well knew that, in this case, my services were not wanted, least of all by the dying
woman.

Upon leaving the Residency, I returned to Tavi's
for supper; I had taken my meals with his family
ever since coming to Manukura. I found him alone
in the store.

"You have heard, Doctor?" he asked. "Mama
Rua is going. Father Paul has been sent for. She
will not live through the night."

Tavi's wife, Marunga, came in at this moment.
She had just returned from Mama Rua's house
and told us that, because of the storm, they had
taken the old woman to the chief's house; her own
small dwelling was not felt to be safe in such a

wind. The rising storm, the expected death, and the fact that Hitia, their married daughter, was nearly at the point of confinement, made Marunga more than usually garrulous. Hitia had had certain warnings an hour or two earlier. This was her first baby; she was a little frightened, and believed the pains signalized the child's immediate birth. Under these conditions, Tavi and I made a hasty meal. I examined the girl, who lived with her parents, and made sure that there was no immediate need for me. I had her mother put some kettles of water on to boil; then Tavi and I set out for the chief's house.

It was a boisterous night and no mistake! The narrow beam from my flash lamp seemed to make the surrounding gloom the more profound. The palms were thrashing furiously in the gusts, and fronds and clusters of nuts came thumping down on all sides; we narrowly missed being hit half a dozen times. Most of the village was gathered at the chief's; little groups crouched in the darkness, in the lee of Fakahau's cement reservoir, or in the shelter of the house itself. Two kerosene lamps on the south verandah flickered and flared, casting leaping shadows across the roadway, and a bright light burned in the state bedroom.

Terangi's mother was lying there, under a *tifaifai* spotless and freshly ironed. She looked no larger than a child in that immense bed. Tavi and I tiptoed up the steps to the verandah. Madame de Laage was already present, the chief having sent for her. The wide porch was thronged with friends and relatives, waiting in deep silence. I had a glimpse of Father Paul in his robes, beside the bed, and presently we heard his voice, rising above the sounds of wind and sea: "Repeat after me . . . 'I confess to Almighty God—to blessed

Mary, ever Virgin—to blessed Michael the Arch-angel—to blessed John the Baptist—to the holy apostles Peter and Paul. . . .' "

The words of that solemn ritual, heard under those circumstances, on an island so far removed from the ancient home of the Christian faith, made a bizarre impression upon me. We could hear, by snatches, Father Paul's voice, but Mama Rua's responses, if any were made, were lost. So strong in me was the doubting European that, even at that moment, I could not share the belief of the hushed throng of villagers, waiting for the end. Nevertheless, within an hour's time the end had come.

Chapter
10

My house was a tongue-and-groove cottage not far from the chief's. It was cozy enough in my bedroom, with the lamp burning and the windows closed, although the frail building shook with each gust of wind. I blew out the lamp at ten and made an effort to sleep, but my thoughts returned to Mama Rua. Was it possible that the minds of primitive people possessed a power over the body that our harassed civilized minds had lost? Like most white men in this part of the world, I had been witness to certain events difficult to explain. When the chief of Amanu lost his life in a reef boat which overturned in the breakers, the people of Manukura knew of his death and all the attendant circumstances a month before the schooner brought the news. I can hazard no opinion as to how this was communicated; I can only vouch for the fact. Strange divinations were of fairly common occurrence, but Mama Rua's death impressed me above and beyond this kind of thing. That a human being, apparently in normal health, should be able to die merely by wishing it shocked as well as irritated the medical man in me.

From Terangi's mother my thoughts wandered to her unfortunate son. In those days I knew nothing of the cave on Motu Tonga. I shared de

Laage's opinion that Terangi had slipped away in the night and made off to leeward. Poor devil! By this time he was either ashore at some island where he was certain to be caught, or drowned, together with his wife and child. I inclined to the latter possibility, and even went so far as to hope, for his sake, that it might be true. Presently I got up, lit my lamp once more, and took down the dullest novel I possessed.

It was past three when I awoke. I opened the door which gave on the south verandah and perceived at once that the wind had increased. The moon was well past the meridian—now bright, now dimmed by scudding clouds. Between the gusts I heard wild bursts of singing. They were holding a wake for Mama Rua as they always did for the dead.

I dressed, blew out my lamp, and returned to the chief's house, keeping an anxious eye on the bending, thrashing palms. The old woman, dressed in a gown of black satin with a mother-of-pearl brooch at her breast, lay in state in the chief's *salon*. The candles burning at her head and feet guttered and flared in the eddies of wind that found their way through the cracks under the doors. None but the watchers were in the room: Mata, the chief's wife, a middle-aged woman who was a niece of Mama Rua, and two grandmothers with snow-white hair. Fakahau's plush-upholstered chairs were ranged in their customary places along the walls; the watchers sat cross-legged on the floor, on either side of the bier. The other people were in the rooms beyond and the leeside verandah was packed. It was here the singers sat, in two long lines, their faces dimly illuminated by two lanterns hanging overhead. Sleeping children lay with their heads in their mothers' laps, and some of the women suckled babies as they sang. One could feel the earnestness of the singers and the solemn pleasure they took in carrying out the dead woman's wishes with respect to these last rites.

You have not yet heard native singing. The taste for it must be acquired, no doubt. I well remember my first experience of it, aboard Nagle's schooner on a bright starlit night far out at sea. There were thirty or forty Tuamotu folk, both men and women, aboard, going to a native festival at Makemo. One evening they gathered on the forward deck, and of a sudden broke into one of their *pari pari fenua*—the ancient songs of the land. I am, perhaps, rather susceptible to the emotions stirred by music. On this occasion I was not able to decide what the emotions were. Astonishment bordering upon incredulity was, I fancy, foremost; never before had I heard singing in the least resembling this. Beyond anything else Polynesian it convinced me of the centuries of isolation from other branches of the human family that must have been necessary to evolve anything so unique. Their harmonies, at first, are more than strange to European ears, but they have an intricate beauty of their own which becomes more and more fascinating the oftener one hears it. At least, so it has been in my case. I doubt whether such music could be written in our notation. I know that Madame de Laage, who was a thoroughly competent musician, made many efforts to take down some of the Manukura songs, and at last gave up the attempt as hopeless.

Manukura was celebrated throughout the Archipelago, both for its songs and for its singers. Many of the people, the men in particular, had magnificent voices, but all could sing and sing well. They had an extraordinary ear for pitch. No instrument of any kind accompanied the voices, but they could begin and carry through one of their long choruses without the slightest flaw in key.

The singing went on throughout the night, now plaintive, now wildly exultant, each hymn ending in the same fashion, with a deep humming of the basses, brought to an abrupt and simultaneous stop, followed by a long-drawn exhalation of breath, like a sigh, in which both men and women joined. All this while the wind was making the house tremble and the roar of the surf along the northern reefs was deeper and louder than I had ever before heard it; the ground shook under our feet at the impact of the seas. During one of the intervals I spoke of these portents to Fakahau. He answered me absent-mindedly. Like the other singers, he was rapt out of himself, stirred by the emotions evoked by these ancient songs of his race.

Dawn was breaking when Madame de Laage returned. When she had paid her respects to the dead, she came to where I was sitting.

"I'm becoming frightened, Doctor," she said, in a low voice. She smiled as she spoke, but I could see that she was seriously worried. "Do you know what the barometer reads? Twenty-eight seventy! And the wind is growing stronger every minute."

The news of the barometer gave me a shock that I took care to conceal. In these latitudes, the glass varies from 30:15 down to 29:70, the latter during the rainy season when the wind comes from the northwest. It now stood a full inch lower, and the weather was not westerly, but north to northeast. I would have been much easier in mind had the wind shifted one way or the other, for that would have been a sign that the storm was to pass to the east, or west. But it held steady at north-by-east. If a hurricane were on the way, it was headed straight for Manukura.

The singing came to an end as Father Paul appeared, followed by two young men bearing a coffin of rough pine boards over which had been tacked a cotton sheet. When the body had been laid in it, the father placed a crucifix in the cold hands and made a sign to the chief. All Manukura filed into the room, each man and women bidding Mama Rua farewell. None were dry-eyed and several of the older women wept in the Biblical sense, lifting up their voices. The pallbearers then shouldered the coffin and led the procession to the church. A more ominous-looking daybreak I have never seen. The clouds streaming southward were of a dull greenish purple shading to gray where they veiled the rising sun. As we entered the church the bell began to toll: a sound faint and solemn, snatched away by the wind. When the brief service was over we set out for the burial ground on the outer beach.

It was as much as we could do to make our way to windward against that mighty torrent of air; nevertheless, all came, the young people helping the old. Another song was sung as Mama Rua was lowered into her grave, but standing to windward I could scarcely hear the voices, and for the moment I had eyes and ears for nothing but the sea. The spray came flying down wind in sheets that drenched us like rain, concealing the reef for long moments, but when it cleared we had glimpses of long gray ridges running in at an appalling height, thundering across the reef and up the beach far beyond high-water mark. Where we stood we were scarcely two feet above the level reached by those huge combers.

A thrill of fear seemed to communicate itself in an instant to that lonely group of human beings gazing anxiously seaward as Father Paul pronounced the Eternal Rest. Although we had heard the deepening roar of the surf throughout the night, none, I think, realized until that moment how high the sea had risen. We now filed quickly past the grave, each one leaning far over as the holy water was sprinkled, in a hopeless effort to prevent its being carried away by the wind. Then the people, as though moved by a common instinct, turned their backs to the sea and hurried toward the settlement. I remained with Father Paul, Fakahau, and Tavi, while the grave was hastily filled. We crouched behind the low wall of the burying ground, watching the seas piling higher and higher up the beach, almost at the foot of the wall itself. Never before had a low island appeared to me so incredibly low, so pitiably insecure. I felt a thrust of fear at my heart at the thought that this narrow causeway, no more than four hundred yards wide; was our only refuge.

Close as we stood to one another, we had to shout to make ourselves heard. Tavi had his hands cupped around his eyes, gazing northward through the flying scud. Presently he turned his head. "Have you noticed?" he yelled. "All the sea birds are gone. That's a bad sign. They know there's something coming."

I had not remarked the fact until Tavi called our attention to it, but it was true. Manukura's colony of sea fowl had disappeared: noddy terns, boobies, frigate birds, all had fled before the storm. This was something that had never happened before during my time on the island.

I put my lips to the chief's ear. "What do you think, Fakahau? Will the sea cover the land?"

"It may," he shouted back. "A great storm is upon us, that is certain. It may be the *matangi hurifenua*."

Nothing could be more expressive than this native term for hurricane, for the words mean: "The wind that overturns the land."

"The church will stand, however strong the wind," said Father Paul. He spoke with a quiet confidence which I envied him but could not share. The task of filling the grave was now finished. "Come," he said. "We can do no more for our poor friend here. We must now think of the living."

I still have a vivid picture in my mind of the village islet as it appeared on that morning, the palms bent far over and their tattered fronds streaming out as stiff as boards in the wind. Perpetual clouds of spray from the reef half concealed the land, and through them one had glimpses of men and women running here and there along the village street, carrying their children from one refuge to another, while others worked desperately in an effort to anchor down their flimsy thatched dwellings with ropes fastened to near-by trees. I saw one small house go skittering over an open space until it was brought up against two palm boles, where it burst apart and vanished in thirty seconds. Several other houses had already blown away and their contents were scattered far and wide over the lagoon. It was soon evident to all that the thatched dwellings would go, and the people were hastily gathering up bundles of their belongings and taking refuge in the church, the chief's house, and Tavi's store.

The air was filled with flying débris, the most dangerous at this time being clusters of coconuts torn loose from the palms. When I reached Tavi's house, a lad was brought in with a broken arm, and for the next half hour I was busy setting the bone—a clean fracture, luckily—and binding on the splints.

I had just finished this task when I heard faint cries from the beach. A crowd of people gathered in the lee of Tavi's copra shed were gazing southward across the lagoon. Not half a mile out, a sailing canoe, close-hauled, on the port tack, was footing it up to the settlement. Her sail was double-reefed; her outrigger, scarcely touching the water, supported three human figures far out on the boom. The man at the steering paddle was leaning against it with all his strength, handling the flying canoe with the quick, certain gestures of the seaman born. An exclamation went up from the people around me: "Terangi!"

It was a splendid sight. Heeling far over to starboard, despite the counterbalancing weight of those on the boom, the canoe seemed to gather itself and rise, skimming the flat wind-torn surface of the lagoon like a racing hydroplane. Full and by as she was, she was footing it at all of fourteen knots.

Close to the pier, Terangi gave a heave on his paddle and the canoe shot up into the wind. The outrigger came smacking down; Marama, Tita, and Mako sprang inboard, and the sail slatted wildly as half a dozen people rushed into the shallows to give their aid. Leaving the canoe to them, Terangi waded ashore with his daughter in his arms, followed by his wife and Mako. An old woman took him by the shoulders with both hands, giving a wailing cry as she did so. "Aué, Terangi! You have come too late! She is dead, your mother! Dead and buried!"

Terangi glanced swiftly from face to face of those who awaited him and read the confirmation in their eyes. Others, Fakahau amongst them, were hastening up. The chief, without a word, led the way into Tavi's store, the rest of us following.

To say that I was astonished at the appearance of Terangi and his family would be an understatement. I could scarcely believe my eyes. That was my first view of the man, for you will remember that he had been a prisoner during the whole of my time on Manukura. It was evident that the canoe must have come from Motu Tonga, but I did not then try to explain to myself how it had gotten there, or where Terangi and his family had hidden during our search for him.

A moment later, Tavi's store was filled with the chief men of the island, and the windows and doors were crowded with women and children and the younger people, looking at Terangi with all their eyes. Whatever his thoughts with respect to the news he had just heard, he put them to one side. He raised his hand for silence.

"There is no time for many words," he said. "A great storm is at hand. Our highest land is on Motu Tonga, and the width of the lagoon shelters it from the north. I have come to tell you to reef the sails of your canoes and take refuge on Motu Tonga; but those who will go must go at once. In an hour's time it may be too late."

There was a hum of talk and argument as he sat down. Some were for taking his advice. Others could not, or would not, yet believe that a hurricane was upon us. Presently Fakahau stood up, his deep voice making itself plainly heard above the tumult of wind and sea.

"Terangi has spoken," he said. "He has crossed from Motu Tonga at great risk to warn us of the danger. Let none of you mistake! We shall need what refuge our lands can offer us. The moon will be full to-night. The worst will not come until then. My belief is that the sea will rise and overwhelm the land where we are, but my place is here with those who are too old to be moved. It is for each man to choose what he will do for his family, but let those who will go to Motu Tonga set sail at once. There is no time to be lost."

The chief then sent young men in both directions along the village street to inform the others. No commands were given, for, at such times as this, the decision as to what should be done was left to the heads of the families. Meanwhile, the whole of the northern sky was covered with a black squall that came upon us with incredible swiftness. The wind increased almost to hurricane force, driving the rain before it in horizontal sheets impossible to face. When it had passed, the first of the canoes made ready to cross the lagoon. It contained an entire family, with a heap of food and bedding under a tarpaulin amidships. Half a dozen neighbors held the little vessel bow to the wind, while the triple-reefed sail slatted wildly. The father, at the steering paddle, made a sign to the others; the released canoe bore off, while the sail filled with a violence that made the slender mast bend like a fishing rod. She tore away to leeward, and a moment later had vanished in the rain.

Canoe after canoe followed during the next hour. I admired the courage of those who went in them; nothing could have induced me to take such a chance. But the wind was gathering strength with every moment, and it was soon clear that the risk of the eight-mile crossing had become too great for further attempts. Nevertheless, one last canoe was ready to go, despite the warnings of the others, Terangi among them.

"It is now too late," he said earnestly. "The hurricane is upon us. You will sail her under if you make the attempt."

But the man whose family it contained was not to be deterred. His wife and three children and the wife's father were already in their places. He took up his steering paddle, shouting to those holding the canoe to let go. Seeing that further argument was useless, they did so. The small craft moved swiftly away from the scanty shelter of the land, yawing wildly as it tore over the smoking waters. Those on the beach gazed after it in anguish, the women wringing their hands. A curtain of rain obscured it for a moment; then we caught a brief glimpse of it about a mile distant. As it rose to the crest of a sea, a gust of wind caught the sail broadside. A cry went up from the watchers as the canoe heeled over and capsized. Then we saw it no more.

Chapter
11

After the church, Tavi's store was the most substantial building on the island, and by early afternoon most of the families at the western end of the village had taken refuge there. An hour before, I had gone with Farani, Tavi's son-in-law, to fetch Madame de Laage and Arai, who were still at the Residency. While they were gathering up a bundle of spare clothing, I took the opportunity to consult the glass once more. It was so dark that I could scarcely make out the track of the little pen. I perceived with a kind of horror that the instrument stood at 28:01, a figure which meant, almost literally, the end of the world in these parts. There was no longer the slightest doubt of what was coming.

It was a full quarter of a mile from the Residency to Tavi's store. How we covered the distance I scarcely know, for the force of the wind was incredible. Tavi, with three or four men to help him, was working desperately against time, making preparations for weathering the storm. He was overhauling a couple of hundred fathoms of new Manilla line which he passed rapidly through his hands as he examined it for flaws. Outside, others were chopping down coconut palms on the beach a little to the east of the house. The force of the

gale was such that the trees came crashing down
to leeward after only a few strokes of the axe,
leaving stumps four or five feet high. To these
stumps Tavi now proceeded to make fast a pair of
bridles with a thirty-fathom hawser attached to the
middle of each. His plan was to ride out the
storm, with any friends or neighbors he could
persuade to join him, in his double-ended reef
boats, which would lie to bridles side by side,
about twenty yards apart. They were heavily
built, seaworthy boats, and would hold a dozen
people each. The stumps to which the bridles were
made fast were the best of anchors, with their
innumerable tough, fibrous roots spreading wide
and deep in the coral soil, and to ease the strain on
his gear, Tavi sprung his cables with the heavy
kedge anchors from the boats, bent on in the shallows about twenty yards from the beach.

Within an hour's time these preparations were
completed and the boats left to ride to the bridles.
Then Tavi took Madame de Laage and me aside.
There was no doubt of his deep earnestness as
he urged us to stay with him and his family and
trust our lives to his keeping.

"This will be such a storm as Manukura has not
known within the memory of its people," he said.
"Stay with us, Madame, you and the Doctor! The
sea is still rising. By tonight it will cover the land.
We have room for a score in the boats, but few
are willing to come. They trust to the palms. Give
no heed to them. Come with us, you two!"

Madame de Laage shook her head. "No, Tavi.
It may be as you say, but I am terrified at thought
of the boats. I put greater trust in Father Paul's
church."

Tavi laid a hand appealingly on her arm. "Madame, I was through the hurricane on Manihiki, in

1913, when there was no land in sight from evening to the break of day. Those of us who spent the night in boats, anchored as mine are anchored, lived. All those on the land were lost."

But Madame de Laage was not to be persuaded. As for myself, I was wholly of her opinion that the church with its thick walls of masonry was the safest refuge the island offered. Nevertheless, I felt that my place was with Tavi and his family, for the birth of Hitia's child could not be long delayed. Tavi was too generous to speak of this matter at süch a moment, but I well knew that he wanted me there, in case the child should come. I told him that I would return as soon as I had seen Madame de Laage safely to the church.

We were interrupted by a young man who burst into the room, his body streaming with rain. "The sea!" he exclaimed. "It is crossing the land at the low place! Father Paul says make haste, those who are going to the church!"

There were, perhaps, a score of people huddled in Tavi's leeside verandah, still uncertain as to what they should do. News of the rising sea now startled them into action. They gathered up their children and a variety of small packages done up in *pareus* and set out for the church. I had gone only a short distance with Madame de Laage when we were met by Fakahau coming in search of us. A group of natives were already gathered on the westward side of the bit of low-lying ground I have spoken of that crossed the island from north to south. The old footbridge had already been swept away and a stout hawser was now stretched across the place, as a hand rope, between the boles of two coconut palms. Several young men were stationed here to assist the women and children in crossing. Terangi was among those on the farther side. Madame de Laage stopped short at sight of him; then her glance met mine. I knew as well as if she had spoken what her thoughts were. Both astonishment and relief were in her glance, but when she again looked toward Terangi there was no light of recognition in her eyes. She was determined not to see him.

We had come to that place none too soon. As we stood on the bank another wall of water shoulder-high, carrying with it an indescribable mass of debris, came foaming through the depression from the outer beach. It filled the gully from bank to bank. As the wave receded, draining away into the lagoon, Fakahau took Madame de Laage in his arms and rushed across, the rest of us following him. We squattered through the shallows like wounded ducks and all had reached the farther bank before another wave came.

We entered the church through the small southern door, and the sudden quiet, in the shelter of the three-foot wall of masonry, was startling. Nearly all of the women and children of the island were assembled there, with Father Paul and a sprinkling of old people too feeble to be of assistance outside. The candles had been lighted on the altar and the small flames cast leaping shadows on the walls. The heavy door at the north end of the church had been closed and made fast and several men were now barricading it with bags of sand. The tall Gothic windows admitted only a faint gray light, and lanterns were burning here and there on the benches where the old people sat.

The priest came forward at once when he saw us. He took Madame de Laage's hand. "Thank God you are safely here, my child!" he exclaimed fervently. "I have been anxious. Had you not come I would have gone for you myself!"

After a word with the priest I again went outside, where there was work for every able-bodied man. The native is not an imaginative person, and like all optimists he puts off until the last moment his preparations to meet trouble or danger of whatever kind; but in his casual manner he generally succeeds in being ready when the time comes. The hurricane was almost upon them before the men of Manukura began to choose the palms in which they hoped to see it through.

Both the young and old palms were passed by in making the choice. The trees selected were those from thirty-five to forty feet high, with well-established root systems and no rotten spots in the boles. Men were swarming into the trees, lopping off the fronds with their bush knives, leaving a cluster of stout butts about a yard in length, with a few fathoms of rope tied to each cluster to assist them in climbing into the trees when the time came. It was wild work with the trees swaying crazily and the heavy lopped-off fronds flying down wind. Ropes were stretched below, from tree to tree, which would give the people a handhold should a wave breach over the land while they were making their way to their perches aloft. Life lines were also carried, waist-high, through the groves, and from the church to two giant purau trees, each of them capable of holding a dozen people among its branches.

I had been lending a hand here and there with the others, but the chief now warned me that I must return to Tavi's house at once if I was to go at all. I was of the same mind, and I confess that I little relished the prospect of the journey back. I

ran into the church once more to take leave of
Madame de Laage and Father Paul. The priest was
going about among the members of his flock, helping mothers with their small children and directing the work of the men who were arranging
benches along the wall so that the old people
might lie upon them in some comfort. His manner was as calm as if it had been a bright summer's
day outside; he even made a little joke as he
chided a young mother who had burst into frightened hysterical sobbing. "There, my child," he
said, patting her shoulder reassuringly. "*Fakaoti
ki te oti*—enough of premonitions of death. You
are safe here. God will not desert us." I was
cheered by that quiet, confident voice, and deeply
regretted the necessity for leaving those solid
sheltering walls.

My farewells were of the briefest. At the door
I turned for a last glance back into the church.
The roar of the wind in the belfry, the huddled
groups of women and children in the flickering
candlelight, and the white-bearded priest in his
worn *soutane* moving from group to group, cheer-
ing them all by his presence, made a powerful
impression upon my mind.

Fakahau and Terangi were awaiting me outside.
It was strange, at such a moment, how Terangi and
I took each other for granted. We might have been
friends of many years' standing. Fakahau put his
lips close to my ear.

"Terangi's going with you, Doctor," he yelled.
"Urge Tavi for my sake to bring his family here.
He will be lost if he trusts to the boats! They can
never ride through such a storm as this! Go now,
you two!"

We waited for a moment, watching the waves
sweeping through the gully, each one carrying

earth and sand with it into the lagoon. Then Terangi touched my arm. He led the way at a run
out of the shelter of the church and was carried
half a dozen yards to leeward before he could
bend his body and adjust himself to the force of
the wind. As I followed him, clutching desperately at the boles of the palms, I gave no thought
to flying débris. What I now feared was being
blown away like an autumn leaf. The danger was
real, I assure you. Terangi had chosen the moment
well. Three or four great waves had swept through
the gully, and when we reached the bank, the water was no more than waistdeep. Even so, I would
have been carried by the current into the lagoon
had it not been for Terangi's quick eye and powerful arm.

Crouching low and holding fast to whatever
came to hand, we at last reached the store. Glancing down the road, I perceived with amazement
that the Residency no longer existed. Nothing remained of it save the whitewashed pillars of masonry upon which the house had rested. As for
Tavi's house, the whole of the weather side of the
roof was gone and I expected the rest of it to dis-
appear even as I looked at it. He had gathered his
family on the verandah in the lee of the building.
One of the boats with its forlorn little cargo of
human freight already rode to her bridle; the other
was made fast in shallow water close to the
beach. Watching our chance, Terangi and I ran
for the shelter of the wall. Tavi grasped my arm
and pulled me in beside him. "We were about to
go without you," he yelled. "We've no more than
time." I shouted the chief's message into his ear.

He shook his head resolutely. "To the church?
Never! It will go, Doctor. There will be nothing
left ashore by nightfall."

An instant later Terangi was gone. Before he had proceeded thirty yards we lost sight of him in a blinding torrent of rain.

We dared wait no longer in the lee of that shaking house; the walls threatened to collapse at any moment. My heart went out to Hitia. You can imagine the poor girl's condition with her child still unborn, but hurricanes take no account of our human troubles. Tavi had her well wrapped in an oilskin. He now picked up his daughter and ran with her to the boat, the rest of us following. We waded through the shallows and pulled ourselves over the gunwale, one by one. The mooring was cast off, and with four men at the hawser we slacked away gingerly until we rode to our bridle alongside the other boat. No sooner had we done so than several sheets of corrugated iron, torn from the roof of the store, went hurtling past not a dozen yards above our heads. There could be no more dangerous missiles; men have been known to be cut in two by them. Tavi yelled a warning, but we all saw our danger and threw ourselves flat on the bottom of the boat, between the thwarts. At that moment the land was once more blotted out by a tremendous horizontal squall of rain.

In the midst of a tropical revolving storm, one contends not only with huge waves and winds of a hundred miles an hour and more, but with a considerable rise in the level of the sea itself, caused by the sharp drop in atmospheric pressure. That part of the village islet where the church stood was, perhaps, a foot higher than the land elsewhere, but it was not long before the great volume of water being hurled over the reefs began to gain on this highest ground. What happened ashore at this time I did not, of course, know until all was over, but I shall tell of it here in the light of my later knowledge.

Terangi got safely back to the church. By that time all the people had taken shelter within it save for the chief and half a dozen men who were crouched outside by the southern door. None spoke of what they feared, but the same thought was in every man's mind. They had done what they could. Nothing now remained but to wait to learn the sea's will with them. The roar of the surf piling over the reefs only four hundred yards away stunned and deafened them, and the sheets of spray flying high over the church concealed the land from their view. Now and then one of the men would peer to windward around the corner of the building, but there was nothing to be seen in that direction save a few of the nearer palms, ragged fronds still clinging to them, bent far over in the torrent of air that was half flying water.

Presently their bodies, sensitive to every warning of increasing menace, felt through the ground on which they rested the shock of an impact mightier than any that had preceded it, and soon a shallow wave, only a few inches deep, came licking along the sides of the building, slender tongues of water sinking into the sand around their feet. Terangi turned his head to glance at the chief, who was staring straight in front of him. They waited, each man eager to ignore what his eyes had seen, unwilling to acknowledge that the great enemy, the Sea, had come at last. Another wave followed, only a little deeper than the first, but this one was carried farther, pouring in tiny runlets into the lagoon. Then came a succession of small waves, smoking, hissing, harried by the wind, spreading rapidly fanwise as they advanced, making narrow channels in the sand before they sank from sight.

Terangi leaned over and shouted into the chief's ear: "You have seen, Fakahau? And the eye of the storm is yet far off. The church will go."

The chief nodded. The two men got to their feet and entered the church, followed by the others. The building was raised about six inches above the ground, but tongues of water had already found their way in at both doors and were spreading rapidly over the floor, reflecting the light from lamps and candles. Mothers with their children gathered round them gazed at the sight, their hearts numb with terror. They sat on the benches with their feet drawn up under them, as though they believed that they might be safe so long as the water did not touch them. Father Paul was standing under the altar with a sobbing child in his arms. The chief touched his shoulder.

"Father, the church is no longer safe," he said. "We must take to the palms."

"No, my son," the priest replied calmly. "I built this church with God's help, to withstand wind and sea. It will not fail us."

"Come, Father," Terangi added earnestly. "I have a place ready for you in one of the purau trees. The sea already covers the land and is rising fast. Soon there will be no choice. Those who remain here will be caught without hope of escape."

Imagine the scene: the roaring wind adding its tumult to that of the sea, the water rising, even as they spoke, until it was ankle-deep over the floor of the church. And imagine, if you can, the unshakable trust of the old priest in God's mercy. He was not to be moved, for all the earnest pleading of those who lacked his faith. But he would have none stay with him against their will. He now stood on one of the benches to speak to his people, who crowded close to hear what he would say.

"My children, the chief believes that our church is no longer safe. I do not share his belief. God sees us. Our need He knows. He will not suffer us to be lost. But I would have you do as you think best for your safety. Those who would take refuge in the trees must go now, and may God bless and save you all!"

So great was the people's trust in Father Paul that many decided to stay in the church. It was, in fact, the only possible decision for some of the old people, too feeble to endure exposure to the full force of wind and rain. The leave-takings of that moment, as they were described to me later, must have been heart-rending, as affecting to those who went out into the storm as to those who remained behind, for none of them but knew how desperate were their chances, whether they should go or stay. Those who were to go crowded about the door at the south end of the church as though unable to proceed farther, reluctant to forsake the last comfort remaining to them—that of numbers. It was Terangi and the chief together who roused them into action. Taking up his child in one arm, with Marama clinging to the other, Terangi made a run for the nearer of the life lines which had been stretched from two palms near the entrance of the church to the old purau trees about forty yards to windward. Immediately they lost sight of everything save the lines to which they clung. The waves sweeping across the land were now knee-deep. They fought their way to windward, scarcely able to breathe in the torrents of rain and flying spray that lashed across their faces. They did not catch sight of their tree until they had all but reached it. Thick gnarled limbs branched from the trunk only a few feet above the ground. Tita was wrapped in an old oilskin coat which covered her completely except for a small opening through which she could breathe. Handholds of rope had already been prepared at the most likely perches, but Terangi secured his daughter with two or three turns of stout line that held her against the leeward side of the trunk. Marama was secured in the same manner close beside the child, so that she could hold her in her arms. Freeing one arm for a moment, she drew her husband's head close and shouted into his ear: "Madame de Laage!" Terangi nodded, climbed quickly down the tree, and disappeared once more in the direction of the church.

The scene there was one of the wildest confusion. The roofing iron of the steeply pitched roof was ripping off sheet by sheet, and as Terangi entered by the small door on the lagoon side of the building, the tall Gothic window in the northern wall was burst in with a crash of rending wood and splintering glass. The candles had been snuffed out the moment the roof had started to go, and the only light now left burning was a hurricane lantern that Father Paul had set in a sheltered place under the altar. The chief, too, had returned to the church to give aid to others, having placed Mata, his wife, and their two younger children in one of the *purau* trees. Peering through the dim light, Terangi caught sight of Madame de Laage seated on a bench against the wall. He perceived at once that she was keeping herself under control by a firm effort of the will. Some of the women had given way to hysteria and were moaning and crying, their heads in their arms.

"You must come with me, Madame," he shouted brusquely. "Your place is in the purau tree with my wife and child. It is your only chance."

She gazed up at him, incapable of speech. Taking her arm, he raised her to her feet. "Come," he repeated, and led her quickly to the door. She accompanied him blindly, like a woman walking in her sleep.

She drew back involuntarily when she perceived what awaited them outside, but Terangi took a firm grip on her wrist. "Don't be frightened," he shouted. "The water isn't deep. Bend low! ... Now!"

They ran for the life lines, but had no more than reached them when Terangi saw that he had started too soon. A wall of foaming water, hidden by the flying spray, was sweeping down upon them from the north, dashing high among the boles of the palms. He seized the woman's hands, clenched them on the line, and braced himself for the shock. Madame de Laage's hair, plaited in a single thick braid which had been coiled on her head, had fallen during their brief run from the church. Terangi seized it just as the wave was upon them and settled to a mighty grip on the line with his left hand.

Both lost their footing in the swirl of waters that swept over them. The strain was too much for Madame de Laage. She felt her hands torn from the rope and fetched up with a shock that seemed almost to tear the scalp from her head. Terangi held on grimly, and when the force of the wave had spent itself seized the woman in one arm. Holding fast to the life line with the other, he gained the shelter of the tree.

When he had Madame de Laage well secured in the crotch of a limb twelve feet from the ground, Terangi took his place beside his wife and child. He had done what he could, and now his place was with those under his care. The rain had ceased for the moment, and in the wild gray light of evening they could see for a distance of twenty or thirty yards, perhaps, on either side of them. A dozen people had taken refuge in this same tree, and there were as many more in the other *purau* a little to the west of them. There would have been room for others, but most of those who had left the church put greater trust in the coconut palms. Through the clouds of spray, Madame de Laage caught glimpses of those near by, wedged in among the lopped-off butts of the fronds, and of isolated figures clinging desperately to the boles as they climbed aloft. Some of the people behaved with a strange perversity. Perhaps they believed that the storm had reached its height, refusing to admit that there might be worse to come. The native mind works in curious ways. They feared, it may be, that the final surrender of taking refuge in the palms would raise to greater fury the elements against them. At any rate, many of the young and able-bodied still remained below, holding fast to the ropes in little clusters as the combers swept over the land. Those in the trees peered down at them, straining their eyes in the uncertain light, shouting anguished warnings which were lost in the tumult of the wind. Against her will, Madame de Laage kept her eyes fixed on one group of five small dark figures who succeeded in maintaining their hold as comber after comber swept over them. They could not or would not, it seemed, seek the safety of the trees. Horrified at the sight, she closed her eyes for a moment. When she looked again they were gone.

Night now descended upon Manukura, an hour of roaring darkness which preceded the rising of the moon.

Chapter
12

The two reef boats were moored, as I have said, about twenty yards apart and thirty from the beach. One held six. Ah Fong, our old Chinese baker, was among them, as were Mako and a married sister of Marunga, with her husband and their small daughter. There were eight in ours: Tavi, his wife, their boy Taio, their daughter Hitia, with her husband, Farani, Arai, a man named Kauka, and myself.

By moonrise the rain began to fall in earnest. I have witnessed many tropical downpours, but the tons of water that descended upon Manukura that night were something new to my experience. "Descended" is not the word. It was driven against us and into us like knife blades; like iron pellets. The sides of the boat afforded a little shelter, but even so our bodies beneath our clothing were tortured by the force of it. Imagine what it must have been for those who took refuge in the trees, exposed to the full force of those assaults.

You will understand that we were not sitting up in the boat. We lay flat on the bottom, between and under the thwarts. Arai, Hitia, and her mother were in the bow, Tavi, Taio, and I amidships, and the other two aft. A piece of canvas large enough to have covered the women was torn from our hands as we were trying to place it around them. They wore oilskin coats and lay side by side on a mattress that had been reduced to sodden pulp by the rain.

The moon was at the full, suffusing the clouds that raced across it with ashy light. It would emerge through tattered shreds of vapor, affording us glimpses of minute black dots that were people, two or three together, clinging to the frond butts of the palms. For all that the fronds had been chopped off to lessen the purchase of the wind, the palms were bent far to leeward, vibrating like steel wires to the stress of the mighty force that held them so. Now and then one of them would snap off, halfway up the bole, and the upper part hurtle away, high overhead, riding the hurricane like a bit of straw. I saw one palm top in which there were three people vanish in this manner.

Lying as we did, so close to the beach, we were fairly safe from flying wreckage. I saw the last of Tavi's house go. The walls collapsed and vanished in the winking of an eye. It was an uncanny sight. Before you could have pronounced two words, the foundations on which the house had stood were swept bare. Not long afterward the chief's house followed, with its mirrors, its upholstered chairs and sofas, oil paintings, huge guest bed—in an instant there was nothing left save the cistern of masonry against which the great seas breaching across the islet dashed and foamed.

But the church still stood, and a lonely, desolate sight it was! As though I had them before my eyes, I could see the little group inside, protected thus far from the full force of the wind, but with spray and solid water driving through the broken windows and doors, the children clinging in terror to their mothers as the combers hurled themselves against the thick walls. I thanked God that I had taken Tavi's advice. The building was doomed. Father Paul himself must have known it by this time. Nothing else remained of Manukura village. The very land itself had all but disappeared beneath the seas that swept the islet from the north. In the swiftly changing light, now bright, now dim, only the trees could be seen, and the church with its gleaming white walls. It gave the impression of sinking slowly, as the seas, a fathom and more deep, swept around it, meeting beyond in great bursts of spray. Then it would appear to rise a little, as though buoyant, to meet the onset of the next wave. And all this while, above the tumult of the hurricane, we could hear, at times, the faint clanging of the bell, tolled by the wind. Its tones, remarkably sweet and clear, reached us as faintly, almost, as imagined sound. It was the voice of that night, in so far as things human were concerned, and a desolate voice it was!

Trees were going down on all sides, many with people in them. It was unbelievable that those which might be able to withstand the wind could survive the battering of the sea. And yet the stumps to which the boats were moored held fast. We rode the seas well. The great force of them was broken before they swept into the lagoon.

Rain and sea forced us to bail constantly, and for this purpose we used three brand-new chamber pots of enameled iron. They came from Tavi's store. In our haste in leaving for the boats he had suddenly remembered the need we would have for bailers, and had seized upon the first things that came to hand. They served our purpose well. Being smooth and rounded and provided with good handles, the wind could not tear them out of our grasp. Even so, bailing the boat was work as exhausting as I have ever done in my life. We could not rise to our knees without being sprawled headlong over one another by the force of the wind. One vivid picture remaining to me from that night is of Tavi, crouched and facing aft, his broad back to the wind, taking his turn at bailing. Of a sudden a fiendish gust threw him at full length, but he held fast to the chamber pot. I can still see him so, his face turned toward me, with an expression of incredulity upon it that was faintly comical, even in our terrible situation. His lips were moving, but no sound of his voice reached me. We could only communicate by signs.

It was at this time that a picture flashed into my mind of the quiet, comfortable *bureau* at the Ministry of Colonies, in Paris, and of my uncle and myself standing before the wall map on the morning when he tried to dissuade me from accepting the post in the Tuamotu Archipelago. I could hear him saying: "Another drawback, my dear nephew: those islands are sometimes visited by hurricanes, and from all accounts, they are most unpleasant things to encounter." The words kept repeating themselves in their appalling inadequacy. Unpleasant! But what could my uncle, who had spent the better part of forty years in that sheltered room, be expected to know of hurricanes? He dealt in statistics, not in the naked truths of life.

The nakedness of a hurricane's truth is not revealed at once. You think you are seeing it within an hour after the wind comes, but your experience of the pitiless majesty of nakedness is enlarged from moment to moment. It must have been toward three in the morning that we saw the real thing. We had been bailing hard and had the boat clear of water to the battens. Tavi and I were lying side by side. He gripped my arm, and at the same moment I was aware of something more coming. It was that strange, immediate awareness of deeper menace one had during the war, when, as one lay under an intensive bombardment, scores and hundreds of the enemy's guns were suddenly added to those already in action. Intensity was intensified beyond all conceivable limits. So it was here.

The island, what little remained of it, disappeared from view. Raising my head to the level of the gunwale and shielding my eyes with my hand, I looked sidewise along what had been the beach. There was nothing to be seen—nothing: no church, no trees, no sign of any sort to show that the land had ever been there. In that dim light, with the air filled with flying scud, it was impossible, of course, to see more than a few yards, but I didn't think of this at the moment. I thought we had gone adrift. I believed this in despite of reason which told me that it couldn't be so, else we should have been immediately engulfed. Then came a deluge of rain that made the others seem light by comparison. We bailed without daring to halt for an instant, although the ones without bailers could do no more than throw up the water with their cupped hands and let the wind take it. I was at the end of my strength when the rain slackened and ceased, but Tavi and Kauka worked on as though their powers of endurance were inexhaustible. Tavi was a big man, weighing well over two hundred pounds. He gave the impression of fatness rather than strength, and it was not until you felt one of those huge arms or legs that you realize how mistaken the first impression was. The boat was once more cleared of water, and with the passing of that deluge the light increased.

Presently, for a few moments, the moon was shining in an all but cloudless sky.

Moonlight . . . the full moon . . . what suggestions of peace, of serenity, are in the words! There can be nothing more beautiful in nature than a coral island, on a windless night, under the light of the full moon, but I leave you to imagine the desolation of the scene we now beheld. I looked first toward the church, and where it had stood there was nothing but the endless procession of combers. No vestige of it remained above the waste of moonlit water. The whole of the village islet was like one of those great mid-ocean shoals so feared by mariners, except that there was still evidence that land had been there. Hundreds of palms were down, but others yet stood, with men, women, and children in them. I should never have believed that the coconut palm had such resilient strength. The stems of those that remained were bent in what seemed impossible arcs, but the sea was their great enemy, washing away their holding ground so that the wind could take them. So many had gone that I could now see for the first time one of the old purau trees that stood near the church. It was a superb old tree, with a trunk four feet in diameter, and seemed a contemporary of the island itself. I could make out several people clinging to what remained of it, but at that distance it was impossible to recognize them. The other purau tree that had stood near by was gone.

We lived from moment to moment. None of us believed that we could survive the night, but we clung to life as all animals do. I crawled forward to where Marunga and Hitia lay, fearing and more than half expecting that Hitia's child might have been born within the past half-hour. She lay on her side, between Arai and her mother. Her eyes were closed and her drawn face told me of the pain she was in. Marunga tried to shout some message to me, but I could hear nothing. She shook her head, indicating that there was no immediate need for me.

Something was amiss in the other boat. We saw the men crouched in the bow, trying to pull themselves closer to their mooring. We couldn't at first make out what they wanted to do; then we saw that one thick strand of their Manilla line had parted. I have looked on at many pitiable scenes in my time, particularly during the war, but on none more heart-sickening than this. The break in the rope was not more than ten feet from the bow of the boat, and they were trying desperately to heave in that small length of line. But what could three men do against the combined strength of wind and sea? Had they been straining at the mooring line of the *Normandie* the attempt could not have been more useless. And we could do nothing but look on. At last they gave up.

I was spared the anguish of helpless watching. Hitia's labor came on at this time. Once, during the war, I delivered a peasant woman in the cellar of a shell-wrecked farmhouse, at a moment when French and German troops were fighting with bombs and bayonets for the heaps of brick and rubble overhead. I had established a first-aid dressing station in the cellar only that morning, and there were a dozen badly wounded men lying on the floor. How this woman chanced to be among them I never knew, but there she was, and she gave birth to her child in the midst of all that horror. It was a girl, a superb child. I was tying up the umbilical cord when a bayoneted German pitched down the stairway at my feet. He had been stabbed through the belly. I remember thinking: I shall never again have an obstetrical case under such conditions as these. A doctor should have known better than to make so rash a statement. Life can show a diabolical ingenuity, at times, in varying even its most commonplace occurrences.

Until Hitia's child came, I was able to put aside, as a physician must and can, thought of everything except the matter in hand. I don't say that I forgot that we were in the midst of a hurricane. That would have been impossible, God knows! But I was conscious of a feeling of something like peace—a core of quietness in my heart. You will understand if ever you've had work to do that had to be done, no matter what the conditions; even though you knew that you might not survive the accomplishment of it.

Marunga sat in the bow, facing aft, so that her body gave some protection from wind and sea. Hitia lay with her head in her mother's lap. Few white women could have survived such an ordeal; for one thing, their labor would have been more prolonged and the exposure would have killed them. Hitia's child was born within the half-hour. Marunga was prepared to take it the moment I could pass it to her. She had brought, inside her oilskin coat, a folded cotton quilt. Wrapping the infant in this, she opened her dress and placed it next her body, rebuttoning her dress and the oilskin coat. I had scarcely finished with Hitia when land and sea were blotted out in another deluge of rain. When it passed, I saw that the other boat was gone. No trace of her, nor of those who had been in her, was ever found.

I shall not speak further of the events of that night. There were none, unless the stupefying forces of wind and sea may be called events. It would be futile to attempt to give you any conception of either. When day broke, the sea was at its height, and the only land visible was a mound of coral fragments which had been heaped up among the stumps of the coconut palms, close to the lagoon beach. The mound remains to this day, an adequate memorial of a hurricane's strength. Some of the boulders are tons in weight, fragments torn from the outer reef and carried by sea across the land. Had it not been for the refuge afforded by that heap of coral débris, I should have been dead these ten years past.

We reached it by one of those freakish chances which are the result of the most delicate balancing of forces. The wind abated about seven in the morning, and in a time incredibly short it fell away to a dead calm. I mean precisely that: not a breath of air stirred. The sky above us cleared until it was of the serenest blue, but far away, on the rim of the horizon, we were encircled by banks of cloud that looked hideous in the morning light. A more ominous spectacle could not be imagined.

For hours we had been beaten and battered almost out of our senses by wind and rain. The sudden assault of silence, of profound, sunlit tranquillity, was stupefying. We were not prepared for it, and when we spoke, we still shouted to one another. Tavi almost deafened me by yelling into my ear: "We've not seen the last of it, Doctor! There's more to come!"

I had little doubt of that. Every sign indicated that Manukura lay directly in the path of the hurricane, that we were now passing through the center of it and should soon have the wind again, as strong as before, but from the opposite direction. Meanwhile, our situation was perilous. One of the lines of our bridle had carried away, and it seemed only a matter of minutes until the other would go. We swung at an angle, now that the wind had gone, wallowing over the seas in constant danger of being swamped. Tavi and Kauka, at the oars, managed to save us half a dozen times. Farani and I bailed for our lives. Our only hope— and a forlorn one it was—seemed to be to reach, somehow, the mound of fragments heaped upon the beach.

Then came the freakish chance of which I have spoken. All through the night the seas had been pouring over the northern reefs along the twenty-mile length of Manukura lagoon. This great excess of water sought what outlets it could find, with the result that a mighty current was setting out through the pass. This kept swinging us sidewise into the combers sweeping across the land. This clash of forces, from east and north, made a confusion of waters terrifying to see: whirlpools, eddies, crosscurrents, wave meeting wave at every conceivable angle. Tavi and Kauka were all but helpless with exhaustion when this chaos united for an instant, seemingly with the benevolent purpose of saving the lives of eight forlorn human beings—nine, in fact, including the newborn child. A mound of water like a small pyramid leaped up of a sudden, and we were swept toward the beach. Tavi had his wits about him. He yelled to Kauka to pull in his oar and plied his own with all the strength he had left. Our line was just long enough to permit us to swing, broadside on, against the heap of coral, and the boat was set down between two boulders—set down gently and left stranded there! It was a miracle, no less!

For a moment we stared at one another stupidly. Such a stroke of luck put a strain upon what sanity remained to us. Then we scrambled out in desperate haste. Tavi and I lifted Hitia while the other men flung out the mattress and leaped after it. We had no more than gotten out of the boat when another wave carried it away again. The rope soon parted, and we saw the little craft that had served us so well swept at incredible speed toward the pass.

The mound on which we were perched was no larger than a good-sized room. Twice, during the next half-hour, huge fragments of coral came rolling and grinding across the land to crash into it, but the impacts seemed only to wedge the tighter those beneath us.

We were hard put to find places of safety, for the top of the mound was no more than six feet above the reach of the sea. The mattress was flattened into a crevice so that Hitia could manage to lie upon it with her knees drawn up. Marunga and Arai crouched on either side of her, and the rest of us took what shelter we could find. Through gaps amongst the slabs of rock we could see the foaming water beneath, but the view that chilled the heart was to the north across the drowned land. It required courage to look in that direction for more than a few seconds at a time, for the seas, lifting their backs as they approached the reef, seemed to rise higher than the mound to which we clung. But we had the width of the islet between them and us as they broke, and the brunt of their force was spent before they swept round our refuge and on into the lagoon. A few palms still stood, some leaning far over, their holding ground all but washed away. I counted five in which people were discernible, but who they were it was impossible to say. Both of the old *purau* trees that had stood near the church were gone.

How long our respite from the wind lasted, I do not know. Half an hour, perhaps, although the time seemed infinitely long. In the midst of it there happened as strange an incident, I dare say, as ever took place during a hurricane. You can picture our numbed, pitiable plight. Fortunately, we were numbed in an emotional sense as well as physically. We had a dull realization of the extent of the disaster. We knew that there were few survivors excepting ourselves, but nothing of the pain of loss could come home to us then.

Farani had somehow wormed himself into a hole just below where his wife was lying. Only his head and shoulders emerged. He peered toward his mother-in-law with bloodshot eyes.

"Where is the child, Mother?" he asked.

"Here," Marunga replied, glancing down at her bosom.

"What is it, a boy or a girl?"

Marunga stared at him and then at me. "Which is it, Doctor?" she asked. There was something truly comical in the shamefaced manner in which she spoke. Her daughter's first child; her own first grandchild, and she didn't know its sex!

Nor could I tell her. I must have noticed at the moment of birth, but the recollection had gone clean out of my head. It can't have happened often, in the history of childbirth, that the attending physician, the midwife and grandmother, the parents themselves, have been ignorant of the sex of a child a full hour after it has come into the world. But not many of humanity's infants have chosen to arrive in the midst of a hurricane. Under the circumstances, there was, perhaps, some excuse for our ignorance.

Hitia, who had been lying as inert as a corpse on the sodden mattress, raised herself to a sitting position and gazed wildly at her mother. "Don't you know which it is?" she cried. "You haven't got it! It's dead! It's dead! You left it in the boat!"

The poor girl was herself half dead and all but out of her senses. Never shall I forget the tenderness in Marunga's voice as she bent over her.

"No, no, my daughter! It is here, living!"

Quickly she dried her hands on her hair, fumbling in her haste to unfasten the garments over her breast. She thrust in a strong brown hand and felt her way within the wrappings covering the mite against her bosom.

"A son! You have a little son!" she exclaimed, her face beaming. And then, in that desolate spot, the sea drenching us with spray and threatening at any moment to drown us, we distinctly heard a faint wail. I tell you, it was something to be remembered! That minute human sound made itself heard against the thundering tumult of the vast Pacific.

"There, Hitia! You heard him?" Tavi half shouted, bending over his daughter. "A warrior! A man child!"

I scarcely know how it was, but at that moment we seemed to feel a faint thrill of hope, all save Hitia, perhaps, who was lying with her head in her arms, her body shaking with hysterical sobs. The tiny voice of the hour-old child certainly had something to do with it. If the most helpless of living creatures could survive what we had gone through . . . Tavi, whose face was swollen almost past recognition, turned his bleared eyes toward mine, and smiled.

"You've a good place there, Doctor?" he asked. "Hold fast, you and Taio, when the wind comes again. We'll fight through yet!"

HURRICANE

position and gazed wildly at her mother. "Don't

Chapter
13

And so we did. We survived, but after a further experience of a hurricane's wrath that I shall pass over with the briefest possible mention. It was worse than that in the boat. I don't like to think of it, even at this distance of time.

We had made what preparations we could for the wind from the south, wedging ourselves amongst the boulders until we were almost a part of the mound itself. Tavi sat astride of one rock, his arms around another, bent over Hitia so that he could shield her body with his own. Arai was behind him on the same rock, with her arms around his waist. Marunga had worked her way beneath an overhanging rock that later proved a godsend in shielding her and the infant from the worst of the rain. She lay on her side well wrapped in the oilskin coat. Taio and I crouched in the same niche made by two flat slabs leaning against one another, and Kauka and Farani were a few feet to the right of us.

We had taken shelter on the north side of the mound, where we were not able to see the wall of blackness mounting the sky, but the swiftly fading light warned us of what was coming. Wind and rain struck us at the same instant, and now we suffered everything that those in the trees had been exposed to. I soon reached the point of half-strangled, stupefied exhaustion when my only wish was that the agony might end, one way or another. An hour must have passed before there was the least slackening of the deluge. Meanwhile, the hurricane from the south, encountering the sea from the north, aroused a chaos of waters beyond anything I had imagined as possible. Pyramids of water leaped up, crashed against one another, subsided, and rose again. Once our mound was swept clean over by such a wave, and Arai would have been carried with it had not Tavi reached back and grasped her by the hair. I doubt whether we could have survived another such assault.

By the middle of the afternoon, we knew that we had seen the worst, and at nightfall the hurricane left us, moving southward like the monster it was, in search of new lands to lay waste. The stars came out in a cloudless sky, and when the moon, one night past the full, rose, its mild light revealed as pitiable a scene of desolation as could have been found the world over. One might well have said that Manukura had ceased to exist. The village islet, certainly, had been destroyed as a habitation for man. From our mound of rocks we looked down upon . . . upon . . . what shall I call that moon-blanched corpse of an island? It bore no resemblance to the place we had known. Nothing remained to show where the village had been. The sea had half devoured the land itself, and what had been one islet was now two, divided by a channel swept clean to the reef bed, and a full fifty yards wide.

The few tortured coconut palms that had survived could not have been more spent with the struggle than ourselves. Not a soul was to be seen in any of them. Their forlorn attitudes were like

our own. But we lived, and never had the gift of
life seemed more precious to me than at the moment when I knew, definitely, that it was still
mine to enjoy; that the word "tomorrow" once
more possessed a meaning for me. I knew where
I should be upon some early "tomorrow," the
earliest available: upon a vessel bound for Tahiti,
where I would immediately apply for a transfer
of post. No more coral islands for me—never, never again! How quickly one forgets!

Not one of those in Tavi's boat was lost. The
miracle was that Hitia's child survived. The grandmother was to be thanked for that, and Tavi's
sou'wester, which had covered them both.

We were marooned on the mound for some
hours after the wind left us, for a great surf still
bombarded the reef. It was impossible to stretch
our cramped limbs; nevertheless, Hitia and Arai
slept, as did Farani and Taio. When exhausted, the
young can take their rest no matter what the conditions.

At last, Tavi, Kauka, and I climbed slowly down
from our refuge. The water was still knee-deep
in places, but the sea was fast subsiding and the
land—what remained of it—gradually emerged.
We made our way slowly, in silence, along the lagoon beach, over barricades of prostrate palm
trunks, spongy fronds, coral fragments and débris
indescribable, peering around us hesitatingly,
afraid of what we might find caught in the wreckage under our feet. We had not gone far when we
came upon the first victim of the sea, and a grue-
somely comic one it was. A fat pig had been left
stranded against one of the few remaining foun-
dation posts of Tavi's store. Halfway over its head
was wedged a metallic funeral wreath such as Tavi
had kept on display among his varied merchan-

dise, with the beaded inscription upon it: *"Priez pour Lui."* Kauka was the first to see it, and somehow, we were not able to summon up even a smile at the sight. We were too weary, too appalled by the silence and desolation of the place, to appreciate the sardonic humor of a hurricane.

I was even too weary to be hungry, although we had not tasted food since the early morning of the previous day. Not so my companions. The Polynesian attitude toward food is a wholesome one: emotions are not permitted to interfere with meals. Tavi and Kauka made a careful search of the region where the store had stood, and at last found a case of tinned beef half buried in the sand. One end had been splintered open, but there remained more than two dozen tins. We returned to the others with this prize.

Tavi had matches in a waterproof tin, but the wreckage about us was too sodden to permit the building of a fire. We set to work clearing a place where we might at least stretch out on the sand; then we climbed the mound once more, where Marunga was the only one awake. Her whole thought was centered upon the grandchild against her bosom. When we had helped her down, we returned for the others. They lay in the same huddled positions, and hard work we had to rouse them. Tavi carried Hitia down on his back. The girl showed superb courage. Not a whimper had come from her in all this time except for the moment when she thought her child was dead.

We gathered around Kauka, who was opening the tins of beef with his clasp knife. The smell of the meat roused my appetite, then. We ate in silence, ravenously, like animals—there was a full pound tin for each. The moment we had finished, the younger ones stretched out on the sand, lying close together for warmth, and, for all their wet clothing, immediately fell asleep again. Marunga was desperately weary, but she would not sleep lest she might injure the baby, nor would she let anyone else hold him. Tavi, Kauka, and I sat side by side, saying little, and that little in hushed voices. Before us lay the moonlit lagoon, but not the peaceful reef-protected lake of numberless nights of the past. It seemed to be stirred to its depths, and still felt the conflicting forces that had harried it for so long; but these were fast uniting in one: a mighty boiling current sweeping westward through the pass, carrying wreckage that had been scattered over the twenty-mile extent of the lagoon. Trees, boards, fronds, countless thousands of coconuts, rushed by and on to the open sea at a speed that made our bleared eyes dizzy. What else the torrent carried with it we were mercifully spared the sight of.

I was on the point of dozing, my forehead resting on my updrawn knees, when I was roused by a cry that sent the blood tingling to the roots of my hair. It came from the eastward, very faint, as though from a vast distance, but it was the unmistakable halloo of a human voice. Marunga crouched beside us with a moan of fear. Old Kauka shivered and moved closer to Tavi, who had raised his head at the sound, gazing in the direction from which it seemed to come. The thunder of the surf was all but incessant, but in a momentary silence between the long-drawn roar of the combers, we again heard that faint, eerie call. It might have been the voice of some ancient spirit of the land, wailing over the new desolation.

"A specter, perhaps," Kauka whispered shakily.

We waited, listening with all our ears, and presently heard it once more. Tavi scrambled to his feet. "No," he said. "It is a man. Come!"

Up to this time it had not occurred to any of us that there might be other survivors on the islet. No one, we thought, save on the pile of boulders that had sheltered us, could have survived the turmoil of waters that followed the shift of wind to the south. We had seen none in the few standing palms visible from where we were, and I scarcely need say that no trees had since been left unexamined on that part of the islet accessible to us. There were not more than a score of them all told.

We followed Tavi in the bright moonlight eastward to the wide channel that now divided the islet. It was brimming to the banks, and the current running through from seaward would have been too powerful for the strongest swimmer. We followed the bank toward the outer beach, hoping to find a possible crossing place, but there was none. There was nothing to do but wait until the sea should subside still further.

Meanwhile, we had called out again and again, and at last we heard an answering hail, and spied a forlorn figure with a child in one arm. At that distance we could not make out who it was, nor was it possible, owing to the surf, to carry on even the briefest of shouted conversations. I returned to fetch my small medicine kit and informed Marunga of what we had seen. Then I rejoined Tavi and Kauka, but dawn was breaking before we could venture to cross the gully. Tavi went first, holding my kit above his head with one hand. We could wade part way; then it was necessary to swim, and Kauka and I were all but carried into the lagoon before we gained the opposite bank.

A man, his wife, and their five-year-old son were there. His left arm was broken above the elbow, and the woman, who was barely conscious, had been wounded by flying débris. The child was uninjured. They had gone through the storm in a coconut palm which the father pointed out to us. It had been so nearly uprooted by the sea that it now leaned with its top not a dozen feet above the ground. I gave both the father and mother a stiff tot of brandy and would have administered first-aid at once. But he knew of three others still in the palms, two of them certainly alive, but too weak to descend. "We can wait," he said dully. "The others first."

We soon found them, for there were few palms to examine. One was a middle-aged woman, who replied to our hails in a faint voice. Kauka climbed up to her and lowered her by the rope with which she had been lashed to the tree. She was unhurt, but in a pitiable state of exhaustion. The second was a young man who had been shockingly wounded on the foundations of a house, when a wave had dashed him from one of the life lines. Nevertheless, he had succeeded in making his way to a palm and climbed it. He was in great pain when we got him down. In a third we found a woman and her small son, both dead from exposure. The lad, who was about three years old, had been made fast to his mother by the long braids of her hair. Kauka lowered them to us; then we heard him give an exclamation of dismay. He came quickly down the palm bole, holding to the dead woman's rope with one hand and braking himself with his bare feet. In his right hand he held one of the closed baskets of plaited fronds called *oini*. We gathered round as he opened it. Snugly wrapped in a bit of blanket with an outer covering of oil-cloth lay a child of four or five months, sleeping as peacefully as though in its mother's arms.

"It was made fast to a frond butt," Kauka said, brokenly. "I thought it was a basket of food and was about to throw it down!"

These six were the only survivors we found, making, with ourselves, fifteen in all. Manukura's population had been one hundred and fifty-six. Of this number, between twenty and thirty had gone to Motu Tonga, but of all those on the village islet, six score at least, only these few remained.

I had enough to do during the next few hours. We gathered the wounded on a stretch of level sand near the beach, and after a deal of whittling and shaving with a clasp knife, a fire was kindled and we soon had a good blaze going. I got to work, dressing, bandaging, and setting broken bones, with Tavi as my able assistant. We had just finished our task when Kauka called our attention to a sea bird circling over the lagoon, so high that we could scarcely make it out. It was the first we had seen since the storm, and we watched it soaring back and forth as though in search of the green land that had once been its home.

"Shouldn't wonder if it was one of my own tame birds," said Tavi, shading his eyes as he gazed upward. He walked to a spit of beach and stood there, uttering a peculiar high-pitched call as he waved his arm back and forth over his head. The bird dived steeply, and we soon perceived it to be a man-o'-war hawk.

"It's mine," said Tavi, as he caught sight of a red streamer fluttering out from its wing; "the one I sent with the *Katopua*."

The great bird came sailing in across the lagoon to perch on Tavi's outstretched arm.

"So it is!" Kauka exclaimed. "He's brought

a message with him. There's something tied to his leg."

It was a tiny cylinder enclosed in a scrap of oil-cloth. Tavi drew out the bit of paper and passed it to me. The message was in de Laage's hand, addressed to his wife, and was headed: "Off Hao, Two a.m. March 21st."

"A hurricane is coming," de Laage had written. "Captain Nagle believes the center will pass close to Manukura. It may reach you tonight. Inform the chief at once. He will know what measures to take. Place yourself under his orders. Take care of yourself for my sake, and have no fears for us. We are hove-to in the lee of the land."

Tavi translated the message for Kauka.

"He's a poor messenger, your bird," Kauka remarked, grimly, after a moment of silence.

"He knew better than to try to fly home in the teeth of such a wind," said Tavi. "More than likely he's been all the way to Tahiti since he left the *Katopua*. Sea birds will make for the high islands if they can't fly out of a hurricane."

" 'In the lee of Hao,' " Kauka repeated, in a puzzled voice. "What would Captain Nagle be doing there?"

I was thinking of the same thing. Hao had a fine pass into the lagoon, and the obvious thing, it seemed to me, would have been to anchor inside.

"I see how it was," said Tavi. "They must have left Amanu for Hao and got there too late to risk going in. There would have been a great sea breaking across the passage by that time. So they went round to the lee and hove-to outside. . . . Where will they be now?" he added, shaking his head. "There would have been no lee to the south of the island after the wind shifted."

"They're lost," said Kauka. "Good boat that

she is, no schooner could have lived through it. Aye, lost with all hands, and so we'll find, sooner or later."

That was my belief, but Tavi would not give up hope. "Captain Nagle's no ordinary seaman," he said. "He's been through two hurricanes that I know of; not as bad as this one, but bad enough! He'll have put out oil bags. No, there's a chance. If any skipper could ride it out, he could."

Tavi clung to every shred of hope that had any justification in reason, and heartened the others in every way possible. He was a tower of strength to all of us. I don't know what we should have done without him during those first days after the storm. He had cause enough for anguish of mind. Besides his son, Mako, lost in the other reef boat, a score of near relatives were gone: a younger brother, two married sisters, with their families—cousins, nephews, nieces; but he kept his grief locked in his heart. Mako had been the apple of his father's eye, but he never spoke of him. If ever he gave way to his feelings it was not in the presence of the others. Marunga was as brave as her husband. She, too, was related, by blood or marriage, to half the families of Manukura, and bitterly she must have mourned for them in secret. But no one saw her grief. It was fortunate for her that she had her daughter and the tiny grandchild to cherish at this time. Arai was the most pitiable of the survivors. For more than a week the poor girl was half out of her senses and went here and there, searching for the body of Madame de Laage.

After the sea went down, we gathered on the east side of the old gully, and made our camp near the place where Father Paul's garden had been. That green shaded place, the work of nearly half a century, had been wholly destroyed; not one of

the old priest's fruit trees remained; but owing
to the wall that had enclosed it, the earth had not
been washed away there to the same extent as
elsewhere.

Father Paul's body was among those we recovered. It lay half buried in the sand at the northeast
corner of the church, or what had been the church:
no more than an angle of broken masonry, a foot
or two high. We buried him as near as we could
to the spot he had long before chosen as his resting
place. All those who could took part in the simple
service. Marunga then wept for the first time. She
sat on the ground, her grandchild in her arms, and
gave way freely to her tears. Old Kauka made the
prayer, and never have I heard one more fitting
to the occasion, or one delivered with more simplicity and dignity than his. I knew what none of
those present knew: that the vast evil of the hurricane had not been without its small burden of
good, with respect to Father Paul. He would never
know, now, of the letter from the Bishop. His life
had closed as he wished, on the island he so dearly
loved.

We found the church bell the following day, a
few inches of its rim showing on one side above
the sand. It had been ordered, many years before,
from a famous foundry in Belgium, and had been
the pride of the old priest's heart. The sight of
it made me shiver, for I could not think of its music as I had heard it on many a peaceful morning
or evening of the past, calling the people to service.
I seemed to catch once more the faint desolate
tolling that we had heard in the boat, above the
howling of the wind and the roar of the surf.
Tavi and Farani were as fearful as myself of hearing that sound again. They dug away the sand
with careful hands, making certain that the clap-

per should not touch the rim. When all was clear, the bell was attached to a pole and we managed to carry it to the site of Father Paul's grave. It was Tavi's idea that it should be placed there. A tripod of heavy poles was erected to hold it; then a little shelter of roofing iron was placed over it. Thatch would not have been permanent enough, and this pitiful roof of battered tin was built as a token of respect. The bell was hung at last, and during all the labor of swinging it in place no faintest sound was permitted to come from it; but that evening, Tavi's son, Taio, by accident, I think, caused the clapper to touch the rim. The faint clang aroused an emotion in me that I could scarcely endure, and Tavi threw back his head as though he had been struck in the face. He sprang to his feet and ordered Taio away from the place. The clapper was then muffled so that there could be no repetition of the sound, so terrible for us.

On the afternoon of the fourth day after the storm, Tavi and I were returning to our camp from the outer beach. It had been a bad time for all, occupied, largely, with a search for the dead. Fortunately, most of them had been carried away by the sea, but twenty or thirty bodies had been found caught in the wreckage, and the work of burying them devolved upon Tavi, Kauka, Farani, and myself. Not only humans; there were also carcasses of pigs, dogs, cats, and fowls to be put out of sight beneath the sand. At last the task was ended. Madame de Laage's body was not recovered, and it was on this afternoon that Tavi told me I need have no fear of our finding it.

"I had best tell you, Doctor," he said. "I had hoped to spare you, but you are certain to be asked about her when you go to Tahiti."

I gave him a quick glance. He seated himself on

a fallen palm and motioned me to a place beside him. "There is no reason why the others should know," he said. "I would spare my niece in particular. You know how Arai felt toward Madame de Laage. I believe she would go out of her mind if she learned what I shall tell you.

"While you and Marunga were in the bow of the reef boat," he went on, "at the time when Hitia's child came, the second of the old purau trees near the church was swept away. You must have seen it, a little earlier, holding on by the last of its roots. A great wave tore it loose and swept it into the lagoon. Rain hid it then and I saw no more until it was carried past us, not half a dozen yards aft of the boat. The current was taking it straight for the passage. Madame de Laage was in that tree."

"Madame de Laage! Good God!" I exclaimed. "No, Tavi. She was in the church, for I left her there."

Tavi shook his head. "You may have left her there, but I saw her in the tree. I had a clear view as it was carried past us. She had on a red dress —you remember? I recognized her by that, for one thing. Terangi and his wife and child were in the tree with her. I'm certain of it. I couldn't have been mistaken. I know Terangi. He would not be foolish enough to stay in the church. He would place his wife and child where there would be a chance for life, and he must have taken Madame de Laage with them."

"Were there others in the tree?" I asked.

"Yes. Half a dozen at least. Some of the limbs were above water with people clinging to them— Marunga's brother Petero, for one, but I don't want her to know. They were carried out to sea, that's certain, and drowned there." He rose to his feet. "Well, I've told you," he said. "Let us speak of it no more."

I lay long awake that night, after the others were sleeping. You will understand my horror of the place at that time, my earnest desire to leave the Tuamotu for good and all. Kauka was right, I thought: there was small chance that the *Katopua* could have lived through such a storm. When could we expect another vessel? The Government would surely learn of the hurricane before long and send out to investigate. We might expect rescuers within two or three months—an eternity to wait. Tavi's attitude astonished me: he had resolved to stay with his family on Manukura, and old Kauka was of the same mind. The native clings to his homeland, no matter what happens. As long as there is a palm left and a bit of sandy soil under his feet, there he will stay. Only death can shake him loose from the home of his ancestors.

I was convinced that the inhabitants of our three huts were the only survivors of the storm. We had no canoes left, nor the means of building one, to search the other islets, but there had been no reply to our smoke signals from Motu Tonga, eight miles distant. Before the hurricane, its palm tops had been visible from the settlement, but nothing now showed above the rim of the horizon. If the sailing canoes had reached their goal, it seemed likely that all those who had landed had lost their lives. To far-away Motu Atea, where no one was living at the time, I did not give a thought.

Dawn was in the east when I awoke. Tavi was bending over me, his hand on my shoulder. I stood up, rubbing my eyes, and he beckoned me to the beach without a word. The others were already assembled there. In the middle of the passage, towed at a snail's pace by one of her boats with six men at the oars, was the *Katopua*. Her mainmast was gone; only the splintered stump, the height of a man, remained. Two preventer backstays of Manilla led from the foremast hounds to the rail. Her bulwarks had been carried away all along the port side and for a space of ten yards or more on the starboard side. She looked what she was: a floating wreck. In the increasing light, I made out Captain Nagle at the wheel, and de Laage in his white helmet by his side.

Half an hour may have passed before the schooner was at anchor near our three wretched huts. Not a word was spoken during this time. We stared at the two men on the afterdeck and they stared at us and at the land beyond. What they felt, as dawn gave place to day and they perceived, in the pitiless morning sunlight, the state of the islet and the silent group awaiting them on the beach, I leave to your imagination. The boat drew alongside the schooner and Nagle and de Laage climbed down into her.

Still in silence, they were rowed ashore. The Administrator's face looked ten years older, but I observed that he was freshly shaven. I stepped forward to greet him. He moved toward me mechanically, but with his usual erect carriage. He raised his helmet as he bowed to the others, and then turned to me.

"All?" he asked, hoarsely.

I nodded, unable to summon up words.

"Madame de Laage . . . ?"

I shook my head.

He made a motion for me to follow him out of earshot of the rest. If for a moment he lost command of himself as he walked ahead, he gave no sign of it as he turned to question me.

I told him briefly all that had occurred, and of how Madame de Laage had been swept away on the *purau* tree with Terangi and the others. You will believe that I divulged these details reluctantly, but he questioned me closely and I was obliged to tell him all that Tavi had told me. He showed neither interest nor surprise at the mention of Terangi's name. After a short silence, he asked me what measures I had taken for the welfare of the survivors and whether anything of value had been found among the wreckage. When I told him that his safe had been recovered, I thought I perceived an almost imperceptible flicker of interest cross his haggard face. We returned to the beach, where I exchanged a silent handclasp with Captain Nagle. His arm was in a sling, and although he made light of the injury, I found that his left hand had been badly crushed in one of the boom-tackle blocks. No one had been lost on the *Katopua*. Nagle had no wish to speak of their experiences, nor did I question him about them at that time.

When I had dressed his injured hand, I rowed out to the schooner. The Administrator's rubber-gasketed safe had been taken on board. From among the papers in a small drawer, he drew out a list of the inhabitants of Manukura, made for the census taken a few months earlier. Sitting at the mess-room table, his pen in his hand, and a well-filled inkstand in front of him, de Laage was again ready for duty. There was something grimly pathetic in the sight of him, clinging to a straw of statistics in the midst of this sea of disaster and death.

"The names of the survivors, if you please, Doctor," he said in a dull voice. I gave him the brief list, my own among them, and after each, in his clear hand, he wrote the word, "Vivant." Then, reading from the sheet of discolored paper Tavi and I had filled in with the names the day before, I gave him the long roll of those who were lost. After each of these he made the notation, "Disparu," in a hand that did not tremble even when it wrote: "De Laage, Germaine Anne Marie." There had been three members of the Matokia family on the island, and presently, between two of them, he sat down the name of Terangi, and marked them as lost. When the melancholy task was ended he turned to me.

"Those who went to Motu Tonga remain unaccounted for. We must go there as soon as Captain Nagle can get his engine to run."

"I fear that we shall find none living," I replied. "There has been no reply to our smoke signals."

"We can hope, at least. If the engine is not ready by afternoon I shall go in the reef boat." He hesitated, clearing his throat before he spoke again.

"I sent my wife a message when we knew the storm was at hand. Can you . . . can you tell me if it was received?"

I told him of the frigate bird's return after the hurricane. De Laage listened quietly, his chin in one hand, gazing at the table before him. There was little in his manner to indicate it, but I well knew that, if ever I had seen a heartbroken man, he was there before me.

I was about to take leave of him when Tavi appeared in the companionway. He set down on the floor a well-filled copra sack, sodden with rain and sea water. De Laage raised his head and glanced at him questioningly.

"I thought I'd better bring you this at once," Tavi explained. "My boy, Taio, found it. It's Ah Fong's money."

"You have done precisely right," the Administrator replied. "Ah Fong's money, you say?"

"He always kept it in a sack in the chest under his bed. Taio found the sack in a puddle of water. I doubt if anything can be saved except the coins."

At de Laage's request, Tavi shook the contents out on the floor. I was thinking of my last view of Ah Fong, clinging with the others to the half-parted mooring line of the other reef boat a few moments before they were all drowned. He had been the only Chinaman on Manukura, and had lived there so long that only the middle-aged could remember the days before they ate bread. He had no relatives that anyone knew of, but like all his countrymen in exile, his dream had been to return home to spend his old age in comfort, and lay his bones, at the end, in the soil of his native province. The dream was upon the point of being realized when the hurricane came: he had expected to leave Manukura with the next departure of the *Katopua*.

There could have been no more pitiful memorial to a lifetime of patient toil than the heap of water-soaked currency before us. It would have been lost forever had it not been for a flour sack full of small copper and silver coins that must have prevented the treasure from being carried into the lagoon. Carefully wrapped in other small bags were bundles of notes of the Banque de L'Indo-Chine, in denominations of five, twenty, and one hundred francs. A mess they were, and no mistake; of all the bits of salvage gathered up since the storm, this seemed to me the most useless. But the Administrator had a great reverence for money, particularly for the money of others, entrusted to his care. Before he was done, he had dried, separated, and pieced together every bank note that was not pulp, and delivered the lot at the Treasury, in Papeete. Ah Fong's fortune amounted to between eighteen and nineteen thousand francs. What finally became of it I never learned.

On the same afternoon, the *Katopua's* engine being still out of repair, the Administrator set out in the reef boat for Motu Tonga. He took with him only Kauka and four sailors from the schooner. I had my injured to care for, and Tavi was left in charge of our skeleton islet.

We stood looking after the boat until it had dwindled to a speck on the broad surface of the lagoon.

Chapter
14

I must now go back a little. When the sun rose over Manukura on the morning immediately following the hurricane, his light disclosed a scene, far off the land, as strange and desperate, perhaps, as any to be discerned that day upon the circling earth.

Only the lightest of airs ruffled the surface of the sea, still agitated by a long, heaving swell from the north. The village islet lay below the circle of the horizon. Out on the open Pacific, a long way beyond the reefs of Motu Atea, floated the wreck of a great purau tree. The hard wood was far from buoyant, and though the trunk lay at an angle of forty-five degrees, the shattered roots, as thick as a man's body, were visible in the clear water a full two fathoms down. The lower limbs were also deeply submerged, and lashed to them, in postures that betrayed only too vividly their final agonies, were the bodies of three women, a child, and a man. But the tree supported its living as well as its dead.

As the sun rose clear of the horizon in a sky which gave promise of a still, hot day, the man perched upon one of the upper branches began to cast off the line which held him fast to the bole. He was a long time at this task. His fingers were so stiff that he could scarcely use them. His face was almost unrecognizable, and his eyes, puffed nearly shut, were suffused with blood. The man was Terangi.

Wedged at the base of a thick limb adjoining his own were his wife and child. At the base of another limb a little below them, which now stood almost vertically, owing to the slant of the trunk, Madame de Laage hung motionless, her head to one side. She was held in place by a rope passed under her arms and around the thick stem of the tree.

Panting with his slight exertion, Terangi was at last free to turn a little so that his body might best absorb the life-giving warmth of the sun. Half an hour passed before he trusted his strength sufficiently to move farther. Marama and Tita were alive, he knew; but he feared that Madame de Laage had died during the night. His first effort to speak produced only a rattling in his throat, but at length he was able to call to his wife. She raised her head and turned to look up at him with eyes as bloodshot as his own. With the greatest caution Terangi climbed down beside them. "You can hold fast?" he asked. Marama nodded, and he began to fumble at the knots in the rope which held her. Tita, who had been completely muffled in her father's oilskin coat and held close to her mother during the night, had suffered far less than her parents, but she was trembling with cold. Marama stripped off the child's clothing and her own, to the waist, until the sun had restored some heat to their bodies. With the same slow, cautious movements, Terangi climbed down to Madame de Laage. He felt her pulse, which was still beating feebly. While he was trying to make her position a little easier, she opened her eyes, but without recognition. Terangi shook his head, as he glanced up at Marama.

Their perch was not ten feet above the water. The sea beneath was of a deep, vivid blue, shot through with shafts of sunlight, and as clear as the waters of an Alpine lake. Marama glanced at what was below, shuddering at the sight.

"Could we not cast them off?"

Terangi shook his head. "The tree might turn."

Both well understood the horror of their predicament. The tree floated in a delicate state of balance. Should sharks come to tear at the dead beneath, it might easily happen that the living would be added to the feast. They had neither food nor water. Meanwhile, they seemed to be in the grip of a sluggish current, moving eastward. The nearest land in that direction was the island of Tatakoto, one hundred miles distant. It was conceivable that the tree might fetch up on one of the reefs of that island. Granted that it did, Terangi well knew that they would be dead of thirst before that time.

He climbed to the highest limb that would support him and peered to the westward. The sea in every direction was littered with wreckage: uprooted trees, palm fronds—all the débris of a great storm. Marama, too, was standing, gazing in the same direction.

"You see?" she asked.

"Something . . . I am not sure."

She pointed. "Motu Atea is there."

"How far?"

"Two miles, perhaps."

Terangi made out a piece of plank floating near the tree. He lowered himself into the water and soon swam back, pushing it before him. Then, seat-ing himself on the trunk below Madame de Laage, with his back to a broken limb, he made a determined effort to paddle toward the land. The plank was a stout one-by-six, a fathom long, and he put all his returning strength into the work; but at the end of a quarter of an hour he perceived that it was useless: the tree had not moved ten yards.

Marama looked toward Madame de Laage, hanging inert in her lashings, and then at her husband.

"Will she live?"

"Perhaps."

Who can say what their thoughts may have been at that moment? Both Terangi and his wife were strong swimmers. Under ordinary conditions, a two-mile swim would have been nothing for them, and Tita could cling to her father's back. Even in their weakened condition, with bits of wreckage to buoy them up they would have had little difficulty in reaching the land. But Madame de Laage could not have been taken. To the westward lay Motu Atea and safety. To the eastward, the open sea and the most horrible of deaths for all. If the alternatives were considered, they did not speak of them. They remained where they were.

Presently Terangi spoke again. "Stop with her, you two. I will swim to the land. Perhaps I shall find a canoe. If not, poles to make a raft."

"Go quickly," Marama said, her voice trembling. She handed up the oilskin coat in which the child had been wrapped. "Make it fast to the limb above there. It will give you something to steer by."

Terangi did this. He then stripped off his clothes, handing the garments down to Marama. Each knew what the other was thinking. The chances of finding a canoe ashore were small indeed. Hours would pass before any sort of raft could be made and paddled off from shore, and night might have fallen by that time. Where would the tree have drifted? How was he to find it again?

Tita stood on the limb beside her mother, her sturdy little body exposed to the sun. As her father was climbing slowly down to lower himself into the water, she gave a little cry: "A hio na! Look, Father!" She pointed to the north.

"What is it?"

"A canoe. Now do you see?"

As the swell lifted them high, Terangi sighted along his daughter's outstretched arm. With his inflamed eyes he could not, at first, make out the object, but Marama saw it. They stared northward until the swell lifted it again, and this time the mother was convinced. Terangi immediately struck out, in the direction Marama indicated, glancing back often for bearings on the tree; then he himself saw the canoe. Toward the end he lost it, and treaded water, gazing before him anxiously while half a dozen broad-backed swells passed beneath him. When he saw it again, the canoe was not fifty yards distant, floating bottom-up.

As he came alongside he saw that it was uninjured and would easily hold them all. It must have been carried away, he thought, when the waves began to breach the land, and was swept through the pass by the current. He seized the outrigger and dove with it, righting the canoe. Swimming to the after end, he forced it deep under water, and released it with a strong forward push. The dugout shot away from his hands, and as it righted itself on the surface, a cascade of water spilled out. Then, with a series of carefully timed forward and backward jerks, he sent half of the water remaining alternately over bow and stern before he climbed gingerly aboard. Rapid strokes of his plank disposed of what remained in the bilges. It required little time for him to reach the tree once more.

No word was spoken. The mother and child climbed down and seated themselves while Terangi held the canoe. Then, gently and carefully, he unknotted the rope holding Madame de Laage and lowered the unconscious woman into Marama's arms.

They placed her amidships, pushed away from the tree, and headed for the land.

When they had gone a little way, Marama reached out to grasp a floating frond. She broke the midrib in two and paddled with the butt.

They were close to the breakers now: great oily swells that thundered over the reef in cataracts of white. They backed water, Terangi glancing over his shoulder, waiting a favorable moment as the seas lifted and passed beneath them. With a quick command to his wife, he dashed his plank into the sea. Both paddled with all their strength. The canoe rose and shot forward with the crest of the wave, straight and true through the turmoil of broken water—over the reef and across the shallow fringing lagoon beyond. At the last moment, the outrigger struck a rock and the slender booms were splintered; but they were safe. Terangi sprang out into waist-deep water, seized the canoe before it could swamp, and guided it to the beach. He carried Madame de Laage to a stretch of smooth shaded sand; then he and Marama hauled up the canoe.

It was nearly midday. Gathering a few palm fronds, they plaited and fastened them together with strips of bark, making a small shelter from the sun. They carried Madame de Laage beneath it, and Marama knelt beside her, chafing her hands and wrists. At last the white woman opened her eyes and gazed blankly before her. She gave a moan of pain as Marama lifted her a little while Terangi placed an armful of dry frond leaflets, covered by his shirt, under her head for a pillow.

A few moments later, Marama and Tita were themselves asleep at her side. Terangi sat near by, his chin in his palms, staring out over the sea. After a long time he stretched himself out on the sand beside his wife.

Chapter
15

Those four people—three adults and a child—in their loneliness, with their memories of what they had suffered in common, were drawn together by ties that seemed closer than those of blood. They were as isolated on Motu Atea as though they had been the only human beings left in existence. They believed this might well be the case, in so far as the inhabitants of Manukura were concerned. At the time when their tree was swept away, they had thought themselves the last survivors of the village islet. It was barely possible that some of those who had taken refuge on Motu Tonga might still be living, but after their own experience it seemed foolish to hope.

Madame de Laage recovered slowly. She was so exhausted, so stunned, at first, that she had only a blurred memory of what had happened. She recalled the moment when the sea had torn loose the last remaining roots of the tree, but almost nothing of what had followed. Gradually, in spite of her efforts to keep them back, other memories returned: of the tree, adrift, far from land; of Marama calling to her, as though from a great distance; of Terangi's swollen face and bloodshot eyes as he peered at her from the limb to which he clung.

When she was stronger, Marama told her, briefly, where they were and how they had reached the land. She and her husband cared for her with a tenderness that touched Madame de Laage profoundly. She well knew what she owed this devoted, heroic pair: no less than the gift of life itself.

The sleeping sea, the blue sky overhead, the warm sunshine, tempered by a gentle breeze from the southeast, were those of Nature in her most kindly mood, contrasting sardonically with the wrecked and ruined land around them. Of the many thousands of palms that had once flourished on Motu Atea, all were down save two or three hundred which had been sheltered to some extent in the very center of the island. The storehouse stood at this place, a low building of masonry, built half underground. Its roof was gone, and the sea, washing in through the broken door, had filled the place with sand, but Terangi had discovered, by digging, that most of the stores within were intact. The work of recovering them brought him relief from his thoughts, and Tita was with him to shout her delight at each new treasure disclosed. Little by little, he brought them forth: two cases of tinned meat, a twenty-pound tin of pilot biscuits, axes, bush knives, iron for making fish spears—even a chest of old clothing that had been the property of the chief. He unpacked the garments with stony eyes: dungarees and worn cotton shirts, dresses that had belonged to Mata. With Tita to help him, he dried these things in the sun, and took them to the hut where Madame de Laage reclined on the sand.

It was noon on the third day when Terangi fetched the bundle of clothing. When they had had their meal of bully beef, ship's bread, and young coconuts, he set out, with Tita, to continue his work of repairing the canoe. Tita ran on ahead of her father, her tattered frock and dark hair fluttering in the wind. Madame de Laage was seized with a feeling of almost unendurable anguish as she looked after the lonely little figure. How many of Manukura's children were left? None, probably, save Tita. It was inconceivable that any others could have survived.

Marama, on her knees near by, had begun to sort out the bundle of clothing; their own garments had been reduced to rags by the storm. She unfolded a dress which both recognized; it had belonged to Marama's mother. The two women turned toward one another instinctively. Tears sprang into Madame de Laage's eyes, though she strove hard to keep them back. Of a sudden, Marama put her head in her arms and burst into a dreadful passion of weeping, giving way, at last, to the full, desolate intensity of her grief. With her heart wrung by emotion and tears streaming down her cheeks, Madame de Laage took the younger woman in her arms. Marama clung to her fiercely.

After a long time, the girl raised her head. "*Tirara*—it is finished," she said, in a dull voice. "They are dead—all dead. Weeping will not bring them back."

"We can hope, Marama," Madame de Laage replied. But in her heart, she had no hope; no more than the others. All must be dead. Her husband and Captain Nagle? No small vessel ever built could have lived through such a storm. No; they, too, were lost.

Madame de Laage felt an immense pity for the girl beside her, whom the catastrophe had robbed to such an appalling extent. She had lost parents, sisters, brothers, relatives, friends—the very community of which she had been one of many closely knit parts had ceased to exist, a little world destroyed within a few hours.

That same afternoon, striving to divert the girl's thoughts from memories so overwhelmingly painful, Madame de Laage began to speak of herself. She and her husband had long planned to take a year's leave in France; they were to have gone within a few months' time. Now she herself would go, to live with a widowed sister in Paris, who was very dear to her. Marama listened sadly, holding her hand between her own. She felt drawn closer than ever to her companion whom she loved and trusted as deeply as though she had been an elder sister. After a brief silence she began to speak, in the toneless voice of one for whom the future holds nothing. Casting reserve aside, she told her story as if it had all happened long ago, in another world. She told how Terangi had been picked up at sea by Father Paul and Mako, and of his landing on Motu Tonga. She told how she and Tita had found him there, and of the happy reunion of their little family; of the plans made for their escape to Fenua Ino. Nothing was kept back. She told of the cave, Te Rua, where they had hidden during the search, and how they had concealed the canoe and its contents. The girl of twenty-two spoke like some ancient crone who recalls old scenes and the faces of friends long since dead and gone. As she went on, staring out over the sea, her listener was conscious of the immeasurable gulf which separated the present from the past, so close together in time.

She broke off. Madame de Laage made no comment. Marama turned to her with a hopeless light in her eyes.

"And now . . . what will happen?" she asked.
"They will come here when they learn of the
storm. The Governor of Tahiti will send out the
warship, perhaps, and they will find us here. Will
they take Terangi?"

"God forbid!" Madame de Laage exclaimed, in a
low voice.

"But they will," Marama replied. "Then I shall
have only Tita. Yes, they will take him; that is
certain. Terangi thinks so. And I shall never see
him again!"

The sun was low in the west when the girl rose
to her feet. "We have now—this little time to be
with him, Tita and I," she said. "I must lose none
of it."

Madame de Laage looked after the girl's figure
with dim eyes, as she made her way along the
wide outer beach, crossed by the grotesque shadows of a few palms that had survived the storm.
Marama's story had impressed her powerfully.
She forgot her own situation—everything save the
possible fate of the young couple to whom she
owed so profound a debt. What would happen to
them? What could happen to them? Her heart mis-
gave her as she considered the matter. She well
knew how the authorities on Tahiti felt toward
Terangi. She had seen the letter to her husband
from the Governor. That letter left no doubt as to
the Government's intentions. Terangi was to be re-
captured at all costs, and sent to Guiana as an ex-
ample to others of the Government's attitude toward such incorrigible offenders. Might not the
severity of his sentence be mitigated, in considera-
tion of his conduct toward the Administrator's
wife? It was a possibility extremely doubtful. Madame de Laage saw little reason to hope that anything she might say or do in his behalf would

alter the decision, as to his punishment, when he should be retaken.

He must not be retaken! There was only one way for Terangi and Marama: they must carry out their original plan. The instinct of the natives had been unerring when they chose Fenua Ino as a refuge. After eighteen years in the Group, Madame de Laage knew no more of the place than its name. She had heard her husband speak of it, but he had been ignorant, she was certain, of any land there save the small bird islets on the reef.

There was no other refuge for them—none. Supposing that Eugene were alive, and that he returned to find them on Motu Atea. . . . What would he do? She knew only too well what he would do. He would be grateful to the preserver of his wife, but mere gratitude could never overcome his boundless and inflexible respect for the law. As for saying nothing and conniving at Terangi's escape, that would be unthinkable in a man of Eugene's kind.

Poor Eugene! She felt a fresh pang as she realized once more that he must be dead, and a faint sense of guilt that the pang was not a sharper one. Had she really loved him? No—her feeling toward him had been of another kind: affection, a tenderness half maternal. He had needed her, and she had not needed him. He had been a part of her life, but she was too honest with herself not to admit that her life could go on with no sense of irreparable loss. Now he was dead—drowned. Well, he had not been a forced witness of horrors such as she had passed through. She thought of the moment when the other *purau* tree had been carried away before her eyes, with Fakahau and Mata and other dear friends in its branches, and of the sudden collapse of the north end of the church under the onslaught of an enormous sea. She drew in her breath sharply. That chapter of memories must be sealed, if possible, forever.

Madame de Laage rose to her feet. The others had returned and were making preparations for the evening meal. Marama was breaking sticks of firewood and Terangi was scaling some fish he had speared. Tita was wading along the shallows close by. All at once the silence was broken by the child's clear voice: *"Papa! E pahi!"*

Terangi sprang up to stare in the direction indicated by the child, who danced with excitement as she pointed to the northeast. Low on the horizon, reflecting the level rays of the sun, the peak of a sail was visible, and the upper portion of a single mast. With the light southeasterly breeze, the vessel seemed headed to pass along the northern side of Manukura. Terangi, who had been joined by the two women, stared long and earnestly before he spoke.

"I can't make her out," he declared, with a puzzled shake of the head. "If she is the *Katopua,* then her mainmast is gone. The topmast and the peak of the sail resemble hers. It might be a cutter from Tatakoto."

Madame de Laage placed a hand on his arm. "But it may be the *Katopua?*" she asked in an uncertain voice. "There is some hope of that, you say?"

"Aye, it is like her foresail."

Quickly, Terangi began to gather the materials for a large fire: fronds, driftwood—whatever was closest to hand. He turned to ask Marama for the tin of matches. Madame de Laage perceived his intention.

"Wait!" she exclaimed. "You want to signal her?"

"Yes. Within two hours I will have a boat on the reef."

"No, no! You must not! Give me the matches!"

She spoke earnestly, imperiously. Terangi turned to regard her with a bewildered expression in his eyes.

"You are thinking of me," she went on, rapidly. "Think of yourselves! If, by good fortune, she is the *Katopua*, my husband will be alive and on board. If it is a cutter, you will be recognized and reported among the living. Marama has told me of the plan you had. You must carry it out, Terangi. Go to Fenua Ino! When they come here, I shall say nothing. All men will believe you dead."

Terangi gave his wife a quick glance. The almost imperceptible lifting of her eyebrows told him all that he wanted to know.

"You mean that we are to take the canoe and go yonder," he asked, with a nod to the east, "while you remain here?"

"Yes."

He shook his head.

"If that is the *Katopua*, she will be inside the lagoon by daybreak. All of the *motu* are certain to be visited. I shall be all right. You must not think of that, but go."

Terangi regarded her with an expression in his eyes that Madame de Laage never forgot. "Aye, we will go," he said. "I will make all ready. When a vessel is sighted in the lagoon, we shall say farewell."

On the afternoon of the second day after the one-masted vessel had passed, Terangi and Madame de Laage were on the outer beach. The canoe was drawn up in the sand nearby, ready to be launched. Terangi had completed the repairs.

The outrigger and both booms had been broken, and their sinnet fastenings carried away. The making of new cordage, from coconut-husk fiber, had been a tedious task, but with his wife to help him in odd moments it was at last accomplished, and the new outrigger assembled and lashed with bright yellow plait.

There had been little rest for any of them during the past two days. While Terangi was at work on the canoe, Madame de Laage and Marama had examined the supplies to be taken, but their chief task had been to eradicate all traces of the presence, on Motu Atea, of anyone save Madame de Laage herself. This had been no small task, and it could not, of course, be perfectly carried out; but they had accomplished much. No one, seeing the ruined storehouse, would have believed that it had been entered since the storm. Rubbish of all sorts had been piled in there, as though left by the sea. With palm fronds they covered the tracks of footprints, and were careful, thereafter, to walk on the fronds themselves. Madame de Laage directed this work with the eye of an artist and a realist, and she did it well. The wreckage strewn everywhere by the hurricane had been a great help. There were few spots, even on the beaches, where the print of a foot would show.

On this afternoon, Marama had gone to the lagoon beach, to keep watch. Madame de Laage sat on the sand, with Tita in her lap, while Terangi husked a sea store of young coconuts which lay in windrows where the sea had left them. The other supplies to be taken were already stowed away on board the canoe. To the white woman, they seemed pitifully inadequate: a bundle of clothing, a light mast and sail made of copra bags, axes, bush knives, a spade, fishing tackle, a kettle, a

couple of pots, and a small supply of tinned food.
Terangi had made a pair of paddles from driftwood. They were none too stout, but would answer, he thought.

He believed that the vessel they had sighted
was a cutter and that the *Katopua* was lost. But he
encouraged Madame de Laage to hope that the
schooner had been seen, and went about his preparations for departure as though she might arrive
at any moment. When he had husked the last of
the coconuts and stored them in the canoe, he
turned to Madame de Laage.

"We are ready, now," he said. "There is nothing
more to be done."

"I am glad," she replied. "Have you thought of
this, Terangi?" she remarked, a moment later.
"Your little land at Fenua Ino may have suffered
as badly as Manukura."

"I have no fear of that," he said. "It lies well beyond the path of the storm. But we would go,
nevertheless. We could manage to live."

"It distresses me to think of you in so lonely a
place, and going with so little."

He glanced down at the canoe. "It is enough for
those of my race. What could be lonelier than this
land where all are dead?"

He turned his head quickly to glance across the
island. Marama was running toward them, her
hair flying in the wind. She was gasping for breath
as she drew near. "Make haste!" she cried. "A
boat . . . There is a white man in the stern! My
eyes were dazzled by the sun . . . They are within
a mile!"

Terangi sprang to the canoe. Madame de Laage
strained with the others and Tita threw her small
strength against the stern. When the dugout
floated on the shallow waters inside the reef, the

white woman stooped to take up Tita, pressing her cheek against the child's as she lifted her over the side. Terangi was already seated, aft, paddle in hand. She stooped to kiss his forehead and bade Marama farewell with a quick and tender embrace. The girl took her place in the bow, and the canoe glided away toward the reef.

Madame de Laage stood at the water's edge, watching intently as they pulled the canoe through the wash of the sea on the reef, waited their chance, and shot out through the breakers beyond. Terangi gave a sweep of his paddle to meet an oncoming wave, and she felt her heart contract as she saw the thin haft snap in his hands. But they were beyond the breakers now. Marama glanced back and tossed her paddle to Terangi, who began to propel the little vessel away from land with powerful strokes. Madame de Laage turned away blindly.

As she crossed the islet to the lagoon beach, four hundred yards distant, she rehearsed numbly in her mind the story she had prepared. Her presence alone on Motu Atea would have to be explained to someone. She scarcely dared hope that the man might be her husband. Would the canoe be seen? Half dazed by conflicting emotions, she hurried on. She perceived the boat while she was still some distance from the barren shore of the lagoon.

It was moving slowly, parallel to the beach, and a quarter of a mile off. The men at the oars pulled with an air of weariness. A sixth man, dressed in white and wearing a sun helmet, stood in the stern, scanning the beach through binoculars. She recognized her husband instantly, and longed to wave, to cry out, but could not.

Slowly the glasses swept the shore line until

the motionless woman came within their range of vision. She saw her husband's tall figure grow rigid. The men ceased to row and turned to stare in her direction. Next moment they were pulling at top speed toward the beach, the creak of the straining oarlocks clearly audible in the evening calm. She gained control of herself and went forward to meet them.

The Administrator sprang out into water knee-deep and took his wife in his arms, unable, at first, even to pronounce her name. They clung to each other in silence. Through her own tears, she saw that his eyes were wet.

"Thank God! . . . Thank God!" he murmured, brokenly. "You are unhurt? Where are the others?"

She shook her head. "I am alone."

"Alone!" he exclaimed. He drew a deep breath. Then, supporting his wife, his arm around her waist, he led her a little distance inland, beyond view of the sailors at the boat. They sat down on the trunk of a fallen palm.

"It is a miracle, Germaine! You reached this place alone? Would it distress you to tell me . . . Or later on, perhaps."

She shook her head and began to speak with her eyes on the ground. "I was in a purau tree, lashed fast in an upper fork. I was swept away, and carried out the passage. During the night I lost consciousness. When I revived at dawn, the tree was on the reef yonder. I managed to free myself and make my way ashore. The others were drowned when the tree turned. I do not know how long I slept. The sun was overhead when I awoke, and the tree had been carried away at high tide."

De Laage listened to this remarkable story without a change of expression, holding his wife's hand between his own. He bent over to kiss her tenderly.

"We will speak no more of this," he said. "You must try to erase it from your mind."

After a time, he told her of the survivors on the village islet; and that all who had gone to Motu Tonga had been lost. When the first wave of emotion had subsided, he rose. "Wait here and rest, my dear. I hate to leave you, even for a moment, but I have work to do."

"Where are you going?"

"I must look over the palms standing yonder while it is still daylight. It will be necessary, I think, to move the people down here."

"Leave it till tomorrow, Eugene."

"No—we must return to-night. You will sleep comfortably in the stern."

"I am not tired. I will go with you," she said. They walked slowly to the north, while Madame de Laage told him that the scattered clumps of palms inland had not been seriously damaged by the wind. From what he had said of the other islets, this would be the only place for Tavi and the rest. She halted to direct his attention to various trees, doing all in her power to gain time for those in the canoe. "We have come far enough," she added. "Let us go back to the boat." But de Laage was not to be diverted from his tour of inspection. In spite of his profound happiness and gratitude for his wife's preservation, he felt that there was mystery here. He had seen the print of a child's foot in the sand, and presently observed, in another place, the unmistakable footprint of a man. They passed through a small grove of palms, the once graceful fronds splintered and bedraggled by the storm.

While de Laage was estimating their numbers,

his wife took the opportunity for an anxious glance out to sea. They were within full view of it now. Nearly three quarters of an hour must have passed. Even though paddling alone, Terangi must be out of sight, or nearly so, by this time. The sun was almost touching the horizon and the evening was beautifully calm, though there was a strong easterly swell. De Laage was counting the palms in his methodical way, making notations in his pocketbook. He glanced up, caught his wife unaware, and followed her gaze seaward.

Two miles or more distant, on the heaving waters to the east, a small dark object appeared and was gone. De Laage kept his eyes turned in that direction. His wife perceived with anguish that he was fumbling for his binoculars.

"I am hungry, Eugene," she said, quickly. "Come, let us go back to the boat."

"One moment. There's something off there . . ."

"I saw it—only a floating log. Come!"

She tugged lightly at his sleeve, but he repeated "One moment," and began to focus the binoculars. She waited in helpless terror while he gazed out steadily with the glasses at his eyes. A wild hope came to her that the wave which had lifted the dugout into view might have been higher than the rest and that it would not reappear, but once more she saw the tiny object clearly outlined against the sky.

De Laage drew back his head with a barely perceptible jerk. A large canoe appeared within the circle of wrinkled sea framed by his glasses. She was headed east; a man paddled astern, there was a child amidships, and a woman in the bow, who made shift to paddle with a bit of driftwood. The little vessel with her cargo of fugitives sank out of sight. De Laage knew as surely as if they had been at his side who those people were.

Then he did the one big thing of his career. Slowly he returned the glasses to the case slung from his shoulder. His eyes did not meet those of his wife.

"You were right, Germaine," he said, casually. "It was only a drifting log."

Epilogue

It was long past midnight. The sky was cloudless, and Manukura Lagoon a vast black mirror to reflect the stars. The schooner lay motionless to a slack cable, while the unceasing murmur of the breakers on the encircling reef seemed to enclose a silence even deeper than that of the open sea. Far away across the dark water, Kersaint perceived a twinkling spark of light.

"The captain's returning," he observed. "They've lighted a torch to make their way through the shoals."

Vernier nodded. After a short pause, he asked: "What happened to the de Laages?"

The doctor stuffed his pipe with coarse *scaferlati* and struck a match, which burned with a clear, vertical flame. He lit his pipe and tossed the match over the side. The faint hiss, as it struck the water, was clearly audible.

"Madame de Laage showed no outward signs of what she had been through," he said; "but you can imagine the state she was in. Her husband sent her to Tahiti at once, to stop with friends. There are good solid mountains behind the town, rising to a height of seven thousand feet. Then, when he had established the administration on Fakarava, he applied for leave, long overdue, and transfer to another post. At the end of their year in France, they were sent to Guiana, where he was made secretary to the Governor. He died of fever, eighteen months later. His wife went to live with her sister, in Paris.

"I was acting Administrator on Fakarava when I received a long letter from her. She told me of her husband's death, and how, when he had first accompanied the Governor on a tour of the convict settlement of Cayenne, she had felt that he had been secretly glad not to have been the means of adding one more to the poor devils imprisoned there. That, I am sure, was an unintentional revelation on her part. She knew her husband. Secretly glad! My God!

"After that, writing guardedly, without mentioning Terangi by name, she told me the whole of the story, and informed me that in all probability he and his family were alive on Fenua Ino. You can imagine my amazement. She ended by saying that she was determined to procure for Terangi the pardon he so richly deserved. The real object of her letter was to inquire as to ways and means. I replied at once, enclosing a letter of introduction to my uncle at the Ministry, and advising her to tell him the story from beginning to end.

"Captain Nagle had brought Madame de Laage's letter, and sailed with my reply. The schooner was tied up in Fakarava lagoon for a week, and Nagle spent every evening ashore with me. You will know how sorely I was tempted to inform him of what I had learned. He believed Terangi dead, of course. One evening I came very close to telling him; but, upon reflection, it seemed best to wait. I felt in my heart that Madame de Laage would succeed, but one couldn't be sure, of course.

"Nearly twelve months passed before my patience was rewarded. The *Katopua* dropped anchor just before noon that day, and Nagle himself fetched my bag of mail ashore. I persuaded him to stop to lunch, and as we shared a bottle of beer on the verandah, I asked his permission to glance at my letters. The first that caught my eye bore the official seal of the Governor, a new man just out from France. I tore it open. It contained a full pardon for Terangi Matokia, and a note from His Excellency, instructing me to have the pardon delivered with the greatest possible dispatch—'if such a place exists,' the note ended. 'The harbor master informs me that no land is charted in the lagoon.'

"I told Nagle, then—all that I knew, and handed him the pardon with the Governor's note. I left him alone for a little while, pretending to be busy with other matters. When I returned, he was still perusing the two documents; he must have read them over half a dozen times.

"There was no holding him. He threw business to the winds and we set sail that afternoon. We went first to Manukura. Tavi and his family were still there, managing to live, somehow, on Motu Atea. Old Kauka was with them. The other survivors had gone elsewhere, to islands where they had relatives.

"I had not visited Manukura since the hurricane; you will understand that, for a long time, I had a horror of this place. We reached the island on the morning of our third day out. It was dead calm, and it took the *Katopua* three hours to chug down the twenty-mile length of the lagoon. I need not speak of my emotions as we passed the old village islet.

"Nagle had visited the atoll from time to time out of sheer kindness of heart. Tavi was unable to buy anything and had no copra to sell. He and his family must have had a thin time of it. It was from Tavi that I learned, afterward, of the cases of beef and salmon, the bags of flour, rice, and the like that Nagle left ashore on each of his visits. There was no danger of starvation, of course. There were enough uninjured palms to provide them with coconuts and Manukura has always been a great island for fish.

"We dropped anchor off Motu Atea at noon. Before we had slacked away, Tavi and Marunga were on board followed by the entire population of the island, who made a load for two small canoes. Tavi's smile of welcome grew even broader when he perceived me on deck. He gripped my hand with a sincerity of pleasure there was no mistaking. Marunga enveloped me in a vast embrace setting down a child of two years, the offspring of their old age. While I talked with her, Nagle drew Tavi aside. Hitia and Arai were the next to greet me. I was called upon to admire three children, the eldest a handsome lad of four who had made his bow to the world during that fearful night in the boat. Farani was there, and young Taio, now a sturdy fellow of fifteen, and his father over again. They shook my hand warmly, with bashful grins. I have never been more deeply touched at a meeting.

"A moment later Tavi came striding aft, his face beaming like the rising sun. He was so excited that he could scarcely speak, but he managed to boom out: 'O Terangi-ma! They live, and the Government has pardoned him!' I will leave to your imagination the amazement, the delight, this announcement produced; the rapid questions, followed by the somewhat surprising assurance that Terangi and his family had reached Fenua

Ino in safety and were to be found there now. I was not so certain, but naturally, kept my misgivings to myself. It was decided at once that all of them should go with us, and that we should set sail as soon as a few small belongings could be fetched from shore.

"They weren't long in making ready. It was still daylight when we went out the passage; then the engine was stopped and we proceeded under sail, with a light westerly breeze. There was little sleep on board that night. I went below about ten and endeavored to read in my cabin, but found that I could not fix attention on my book. The voices of the natives came down through the open skylight. The mate and the sailors off watch were discussing with the Manukura folk the adventures of Terangi from boyhood to his probable state at the present time. They took it absolutely for granted that we should find the little family alive and well on the morrow. Old Marunga's voice rose above the others in tones of extraordinary animation, coming now and then to dramatic pauses, ending with a resounding slap of both hands on her knees. Eight bells had sounded when I fell asleep at last, with the voice of Marunga growing fainter in my ears.

"We hove-to off Fenua Ino at one o'clock on the following afternoon. Save for the encompassing reef, the atoll is very imperfectly laid down on the charts. The lagoon is nearly circular, and about nineteen miles across. The afternoon was calm, and the reef itself scarcely discernible in the gentle wash of the sea. The only bits of land in sight were the two tiny islets, neither more than half an acre in extent, with scattered scrub and the vivid green of the pohue creeper along the beaches. The boat passage was close to where we lay, but no no man on board had been inside. Nothing was here to tempt the utilitarian white man, and the natives had always shunned the place because of their legends of some old unhappiness.

"Leaving the schooner in charge of the mate, with instructions to stand off and on, Nagle ordered his two reef boats overside and we piled in. Nagle would deny none of the Manukurans the pleasure of joining in the search. Tavi took command of one boat; I went with the skipper in the other. The passage proved shallow and very crooked, but we had no trouble in getting inside. A mass of coral shoals extended eastward for a mile or more; we were an hour in getting clear. Then, with deep blue water under us, we set out at a smart pace. After a time, the faint line of breakers on the encircling reef dropped away out of sight, as did the two low islets to the south. Propelled by the powerful arms of the oarsmen, we glided over this lake of smooth salt water, which seemed to stretch away to infinite distances on all sides, rippling gently to the light west wind. The sun was well down when I heard a shout from the other boat: *"Te motu!"* We scrambled to our feet.

"I saw the land at once, the familiar atoll landfall: a series of slight irregularities on the horizon, made up of palm tops seen from afar. The men at the oars pulled on steadily. The sun was almost touching the horizon when we drew near the land.

"The islet seemed to be about a hundred and fifty acres in extent, and was covered with young coconuts, above which towered many tall old palms. We rowed toward a small indentation on the western side. A babble of talk went up as we rounded a point and perceived at the head of the

cove a canoe drawn up under a low thatched shed.
'They are here! . . . I knew it! . . . He has sighted us
and gone to hide!' One or two of them glanced ac-
cusingly at my white official helmet.

"At that moment, Terangi stepped out of a thicket and stood awaiting us. Tita now a girl of ten
years stood at his side, as wild and lovely as some
Polynesian nymph. A small boy of three was half
hidden behind his father, who held a younger
child in his arms. What his thoughts were, it would
be hard to conjecture; at any rate, the children
forced him to put aside any thought of escape.
His attitude was one of stern, dignified submittal
to a fate which had overtaken him at last. No word
was spoken till our boat's keel grated on the sand.
It was Tavi, behind us, who broke the silence.

" 'Where is Marama?' he asked, hoarsely.

"Terangi shook his head with a barely perceptible movement. Nagle pushed past us and sprang
out into the shallows. He grasped Terangi by the
shoulders and then embraced him with a hug like
that of a bear.

"I shall say no more of that first hour. We were
all profoundly stirred, and there was much to talk
over, much to explain. The deep happiness of Tavi
and his clan was sobered by the loss of Marama,
who had died in childbirth the year before. Terangi received the news of his pardon calmly, and led
the way in the dusk to his house. Marama's grave
was close by, bordered with white shells and sur-
mounted by a rough-hewn cross.

"We sat long that evening, in the light of a fire
of coconut husks. The next morning, with Terangi
as our guide, Nagle and I made a tour of the islet.
It was remarkable to see what one man could
accomplish in a little more than four years. He

had cleared and planted the entire island and had better than seven thousand young coconut palms coming on. He had found the *puraka* taro of the low islands growing wild and had planted beds of it, digging down to the level where the ground is perpetually moist. His house, though small, was as pretty a thatched hut as I have seen, with its rafters made fast with ornamental sinnet lashings. One could see the work of Marama's hands, and Tita's, in the shrubbery planted around it.

"The island looked so promising, in fact, that, at Terangi's suggestion, Tavi and his family made up their minds to stop there for good, provided that Nagle would let them have one of his boats to enable them to go back and forth to Manukura when they wished. The captain agreed. Late that evening we boarded the schooner, and the settlers of Fenua Ino pulled back into their lagoon. And that's the whole of the story, save that Nagle, poor chap, was drowned the same year, in a capsized boat at Fakahina, one of the worst reef landings in the Archipelago."

Dr. Kersaint stretched his arms wide and yawned. In the silence, the voices of the returning fishermen were heard. The boat came alongside. The native captain climbed on board, carrying a heavy string of fish. Seeing that the two white men were still up, he came aft to display his catch. A sailor followed with a lantern and held it aloft so that its light shone down on the burnished sides of parrot fish and trevally. Vernier looked, rather, at the captain's powerful torso and his lined and rugged face. "A magnificent-looking fellow," he thought.

"You've been lucky, as usual," the doctor remarked.

The captain nodded, with a grave smile, and turned to go forward.

Kersaint rose. "I've kept you up till all hours," he said. "You must forgive a garrulous old man."

". . . But tell me one thing! Is Terangi still on his island?" Vernier asked.

"No. He's been at sea ever since his pardon came. Nagle left him the old *Katopua* in his will. He's her skipper now."

ABOUT THE AUTHORS

CHARLES NORDHOFF and **JAMES HALL** formed
one of the most famous American literary teams
in the years between the two World Wars.
Charles Nordhoff was born in London and edu-
cated at Harvard. After serving in World War I
he collaborated with his friend James Hall to
write a history of the Lafayette Flying Corps.
Drawing upon their vast knowledge of the South
Seas in subsequent books, the two writers began
a long and fruitful partnership that included such
world-famous books as Men Against the Sea,
Pitcairn's Island, Hurricane, and Mutiny on the
Bounty.

RELAX!

SIT DOWN
and Catch Up On Your Reading!